PROPHECY OF HONOR

FRED WAISS

Published by Water Dragon Publishing
waterdragonpublishing.com

ISBN 978-1-964952-77-2 (Trade Paperback)

FIRST EDITION

10 9 8 7 6 5 4 3 2 1

PROPHECY
OF
HONOR

1

THE SLAVE

THE FUNERAL FIRES WERE STILL SMOLDERING, but after four days the flames were no longer visible within the blackened collapsed pyres. My anger, with the flames, had subsided but still simmered within.

The damned Kursh were the focus of my anger. It was not that they had tried to kill me. They have been trying to do that for over half my life. It always turns out badly for them. But this time it had cost the lives of over thirty of my warriors. Brave men and women, faithful and skilled all, had died because the Kursh continued to pursue a course that was doomed to failure.

Besides the thirty-three dead, another twenty were wounded, and almost half of them had sustained injuries that would be with them the rest of their lives—severed limbs, damaged eyes, disfigured faces.

That over one hundred Kursh had been killed in their attempt was no consolation. If the damned sheep rapists wished to kill me, fine, but leave my warriors out of it!

But the business of the Keep cannot be ignored for too long, no matter the provocation. As I stood on the observation platform above the reaping floor, most of the slaves had looked up. Those that had been long in the service of Honor Keep had given a gesture of respect, acknowledging the losses of the Keep. I returned their gestures with a nod, meeting the eyes of several. They then went back to their work.

The large room with its wooden pillars was well-lighted. The sun windows were open on the slanted roof. The slaves worked from when the sun was high enough to provide sufficient light until it was too low on the opposite horizon. At the end of each day male slaves carried the barrels of sugar pulp to the pressing machines in the adjoining building. Some of the female slaves gathered the stripped fibers into bundles and set them aside for others to take for fuel for the fires; others swept the wooden floors.

Then the slaves would go to the outdoor baths where they would wash themselves and their clothing. All servants and slaves that worked in the reaping shed had two sets of clothing, except for the gloves. The day's clothes would be hung up to dry during the following day.

Then I saw her. My anger melted away like the rare snow in the following sunshine.

My anger disappeared, partly, because when I saw her I knew at once that the attack by the Kursh, and the battle, and the deaths of my soldiers had all been a pre-ordained part of my destiny.

But the main reason was because I could no more look at her and maintain anger than I could nurture rage in a field of flowers.

She stood out like a cut diamond in a display of river rock. It wasn't just that she was pretty ... outstandingly pretty, really ... because there were other pretty slaves among the workers. Some real beauties, in fact. The silvery hair, though, was unique. Only the Aelfir had hair like that.

She had looked up also, as had the other new slaves, acquired as spoils of war when the Kursh were defeated. She studied me with curious interest until one of the others had nudged her and urged her to return to work. She'd given me one last quick glance and then bent reluctantly back to her duties.

"Tom, why was she not sent to the house? She is obviously Aelfir."

"Honor, I only suspected that she might be. I have not your learning, nor your eye. That is why I requested your visit. I did not wish to simply send her to you. There was an incident, and I believe she may be dangerous."

"Has she been beaten?"

"Of course not, Sir."

"Raped?"

"Unlikely. But that is why I think there is more to her than meets the eye. There were three of the guards that decided to do just that. Two of them came to me with the body of the third, and confessed the story.

"It seems that they cornered her outside as she returned from the outbuildings. The one approached her boldly and went to grab her, and not gently. She reached up and touched his forehead with her hand. He stopped, stood motionless for a few seconds, and then collapsed, dead.

"The slave looked at them fearfully, they said, and then ran back to the barracks. They brought him to me."

"What did you do with them?"

"They were given their pay to that day and then driven out past our western garrison and sent on their way. They were told not to be seen near Honor Keep again."

"Good job, Tom." I noticed he took the compliment with pride. He was one of many former slaves that had earned their freedom with their performance. My father had freed him, and he had consented to stay after I became Honor.

"How's her production?"

"Terrible. She tries, though. At first, she wept all the time. I do not think it was because she was a slave, since she was that already. It's the work. She could barely bring herself to break the stalks and strip the fibers. Her hands trembled; her fingers barely plucked at the ends of the stalks. It was necessary to speak harshly to her to inspire her to actually do the work. It seemed to actually cause her pain."

"It did, in a way. Her hands are meant to make things grow, not tear apart. She'll be far more productive in the orchards and gardens, and even the fields. Pull her in an hour and bring her to the house yourself. Tell them she is to bathe before the evening meal and be given clean clothing suitable for garden work. I'll have a place prepared in the barracks there.

"Generally, how are the new ones adapting?"

"Quite well, Honor. They still seem surprised that we do not treat them as the Kursh did, and many behave as though they expect the relative kindness to be a trick of some kind. We've reassured them, but it seems to make little impression."

"They will learn over time. But don't relax the guard, either. They belong to the Keep now, and though we may treat them with some respect, they are still slaves. We know too little about them to allow them the freedom of the Keep or the town."

Tom bowed. "Yes, Honor. It will be as you say. Our thanks for your visit. I will bring the Aelfir to the house an hour hence."

I nodded and walked out of the building into the sunshine. I was tempted to take a last look at the Aelfir woman, but denied myself. I'd see her soon enough.

2

THE GARDEN

I HAD TOLD THE HOUSE OVERSEER to assign her to the garden. He was to make sure she did not try to escape, and schedule her meal and sleep times, but otherwise leave her to her own inclinations.

I liked watching her from the balcony. During her third day there, Mother and Heather joined me in the observation.

"Heather, I was watching your bow practice. You are getting faster without sacrificing accuracy. Well done. It will be not too far into the future when we will need all the archers we can get."

"Thank you, Brother," she responded, obviously pleased. "Our mother is an excellent teacher."

"Plus, no doubt, you inherited much of your ability."

My mother said, "As did you, Collin. With both sword and bow, you were skilled the first time you picked up either weapon."

I bowed shortly and grinned. "Thank you for that, Mother. I imagine the many months' worth of hours in practice since has contributed as well to my current proficiency."

"As for your sister, now that she has become at least passable with the bow, it is time she learned the spear."

"I was thinking the same thing. Sister, looks like you'll be collecting some bruises."

She shrugged. "About time, I suppose … but … do you think Lars will mind?"

Mother looked offended. "If he does, I will fetch him a few! He should treasure them! Your father was proud of me when I sported mine!"

I looked back to the garden. The slave girl seemed to wander randomly through the paths, but I suspected there was a purpose to her route. She would touch a plant or a flower, and the change was not quite instant, but it was quick. Also, I noticed that she seemed to speak to the plant. Though I could not hear from this distance, I could see her lips move. The plant would bloom new flowers even if not in season. Flowers would multiply and grow and their colors would take on a vibrancy I'd not seen before.

"She is the one, then."

"Almost certainly."

Heather offered her observation. "She is beautiful, Collin. Have you spoken to her yet?"

"Not yet. There is no hurry. The Prophecy offers no guide to the time we take for this. My intuition tells me that this will work best if she is not rushed." We all continued to watch the Aelfir as we spoke. Her magic was delightful.

"But Turg is striving even now to build his forces. Every day you give him is a day he grows closer to his goal."

"Mother, if the Prophecy is worth anything, it will matter not a wit. If I was to hurry this, it would still be nearly two years before he would make his move. A few additional days or even weeks won't make any difference." I then turned and faced her.

"Or have you lost faith in the Prophecy?" Before she could answer, I grinned teasingly. "Or are you just in a hurry to get rid of me?"

She swatted me on the arm. "Collin! You know better than to even think such a thing! Either thing!" She looked out toward the southern horizon. Some days it seemed like one could see beyond our cultivated fields all the way to the beginning of the desert many miles beyond. Today, however, was not one of those days, and Mother directed her gaze back to the garden.

She had not changed much from the woman I remembered as a child. She was still beautiful though some lines had taken up residence around her eyes and her forehead. But her chin was still firm, the flesh of her neck and throat still smooth and clear. Her hands still could hold a spear and use it well. Her eye was still sharp enough to center an arrow on the target from thirty paces. She had been a warrior for my father when the need arose and for me as well some years later.

"I have lived under the onus of that damned Prophecy since you were born. Actually, since even before I was born, but I didn't know it until your father revealed it to me after your birth. Sometimes I just want it all to be over, and I try to forget exactly what that means."

I put my arm around her shoulders and gave her an affectionate hug.

"I know. But there's no sense in worrying. All the big events were taken out of our hands a hundred years ago. It is only the details that we can still control. And I intend to enjoy exerting as much control over those details as possible."

I looked back at the garden. It covered over an acre, and much of it was clearly more colorful and more alive than before the Aelfir had entered it.

"I believe it is time, though, to make her acquaintance," I said and turned to Mother. "I'm going to have her as my guest for dinner tomorrow evening. Care to join us?"

She chuckled. "Since when does a young man want his mother or sister present during his courtship of a young lady? We will eat in our own quarters for now."

"Courtship? She is a slave. I would not consider 'courtship' to be an accurate term."

"Really? And what other term would you apply to what you are planning?"

I tried to come up with a good answer, but none was quickly forthcoming. Mother chuckled again and gave me a quick kiss on the cheek. Heather giggled "Courtship!" and the two disappeared into the building.

After a few minutes I too deserted the balcony and made my way down to the garden. I enjoyed the walk along the paths. The fragrances of the flowers and leaves had been enhanced as much as the colors and growth of the blooms. I hoped Mother would come here often now. She truly loved this place, and the enhancement would certainly please her.

As I strolled, though, I directed my steps to where the slave was working her magic. I rounded a bend in the path and there she was, her back to me, on one knee as she caressed the thorny branches of a large rose bush. Without seeming to take any particular care she avoided being pricked by the thorns as she touched the branches encouragingly, and white roses bloomed along the branches.

"There. You are as beautiful as any flowers here. But I do not understand why anyone would insist on thorny plants in a garden of this magnificence."

"Mother just happens to be very fond of roses."

She started, jumped up and turned around, then her eyes widened and she hastily knelt before me, head down.

"Forgive me, Master!"

"What have you done that requires forgiveness?"

"I was unaware of your presence. I should have known you were near, and greeted you with proper respect."

"Stand up."

She hurriedly stood, keeping her head down, not daring to meet my eyes.

"Raise your eyes to mine."

Timidly, she did so. She looked me in the eyes briefly, blushing, and then looked away.

She was taller than I had thought, barely a foot shorter than I. She wore a short sleeveless shift and loose-fitting shorts both made of white linen. It revealed that her legs, arms, and even her body were as exquisitely pretty as her face. The slightly turned-up nose and lavender eyes between the high unlined forehead and excellent lips were even more enchanting than when seen from a distance. I was nearly spellbound.

"What is your name?"

She bowed her head again, but I cleared my throat commandingly and she looked back up, uncomfortable with the apparent boldness.

"My Master has not yet said what name he wishes me to answer to."

"Did the Kursh teach you that response?"

She nodded.

"Was pain involved in those lessons?"

She nodded again and her eyes revealed a hint of tears.

"We are not Kursh. When I ask you your name, I want you to tell me the name your parents gave you when you were a child in Aelf."

"Tsha," she almost whispered. Then, more boldly, she lifted her chin and met my eyes. "My name is Tsha."

"Walk with me, Tsha." I continued to stroll along the garden paths and she, after a second of hesitation, hurried to accompany me.

I gestured to a spot beside me. "Not behind me, but here, at my side. Here in the garden, you will from now on consider yourself my companion, not my property. You will conduct yourself in that manner. Understood?"

She walked beside me. She held her body tense, uncomfortable and uncertain. She had found herself in a situation not only new to her, but unimagined.

"Master, if I may inquire, how should I address my companion in the garden?"

I chuckled. "Certainly not as 'Master'! You may address me by my title, both in the garden and elsewhere."

"Yes, Honor. I thank you for that privilege."

"You have earned it, Tsha. Your work here in the garden is magnificent. Much more fulfilling than in the reaping room, yes?"

"Oh, yes! Thank you also for that, Ma—Honor. That work was … difficult … for me. This, though, is hardly work. It is what we are born to do."

"I know. I have some familiarity with Aelf, and the Aelfir. My father traveled there a few times, and he was a great writer of journals and notes. Everything he learned of the lands and peoples he visited he wrote down. I do that myself, now, for my own children, if and when.

"I have been there myself, once, for more than a week. I have some knowledge of your abilities as well as your history, your customs, and your troubles."

As we walked I led us back to the garden gateway. Joseph, the overseer, stood sentry there. I gave him a quick nod of recognition as we stopped.

I turned and faced her. She had relaxed some during our conversation, beginning to believe that I was not simply hoping for an excuse to punish her.

"And now I would like to know more, about your land, your people, and about you. You will have dinner with me tomorrow evening."

I turned to Joseph. "See that she has the opportunity to bathe and dress and deliver her to the dining area shortly before the meal is due to be served. I will send clothing a bit more appropriate for the dining room."

He bowed. "Yes, Honor! It will be as you say. Thank you for the visit."

I turned to Tsha. She seemed in a state of shock, but she tried to recover. She bowed hastily. "My eternal gratitude, Honor! I happily await my chance to repay your generosity however you may wish."

I shook my head at her. "A simple 'thank you' will suffice. Generosity never requires repayment."

With that, I turned and left them. I suspected Mother would have something in her closets that would do. She and Tsha were near enough to the same height, though Mother was by birth and training of a larger frame.

3

ᴛhe companion

TSHA ENTERED THE DINING ROOM exactly on time. Her dress was perfect, trim and close-fitting, yet modest, covering her from shoulder to ankle and the arms to just above the elbows. Mother had sent a servant to get details of her appearance, including her exact measurements, and then Mother's tailors had done a quick but very professional job of alterations. They'd even managed to alter a pair of sandals. The Aelfir tend to have small feet.

The dress was lavender and matched Tsha's eyes, with silver trim that very nearly matched her hair. Mother always had great fashion sense. But the slave girl looked uncomfortable dressed as not just a free woman, but a free woman of high station.

I pretended not to notice her unease and stepped quickly to stand in front of her. Since she was dressed as a free woman of high station, I had the sudden impulse to treat her as such. I bowed to her, then took her left hand in my right and kissed the back.

"Good evening, my lady. Welcome." I gestured to the table and the chairs.

"Mas—Honor. I did not know you wished your slave here for mockery."

"Tsha, again you mistake me for Kursh. I do not mock. You are beautiful in slave's garb. But in such fashion as you now wear, you are so much more. If you dine with me, you are, at least for that time, not my slave. You are a free woman of high station. Allow me to treat you as a gentleman should treat such a lady."

She did not look convinced, but allowed me to sit her at the table. The table had room for eight settings. I sat at one end after seating her at the first place to my left.

As the evening progressed and she became more comfortable with me and the surroundings she seemed to recall when she was herself a free woman. Manners and demeanor long suppressed reemerged in her actions. Though she relaxed, she maintained a cautious seriousness.

I made small talk during dinner, asking about her barrack arrangements, the details of her transfer from slavery by the Kursh to that of the Free People, and about her parents and childhood in Aelf. She was not a chatterer. Her speech was reserved and restrained, yet she answered all questions freely and completely. She was, she thought, about twenty-two years old, though her time as a slave to the Kursh might have passed more quickly, or more slowly, than she was able to determine.

There was one significant bit of information I needed. Already I was planning for events perhaps two years away, prodded to do so by the Prophecy. I thought perhaps Tsha might provide that information.

"Tsha, a question. If I was to sneak somehow into a Kursh camp of warriors, what could I be absolutely certain that I would find there?"

She seemed puzzled by the question. "I hope Honor is not contemplating something that reckless. Even with disguise you could not pass for Kursh."

"No, I am not planning recklessness. Or at least not that kind. But you offer a chance to learn something of our enemy. So, again, what is always, without fail, in a soldiers' camp of the Kursh?"

She answered immediately. "Fire. There are always fires burning. It is like a talisman to them. No slaves may feed the fire even a single twig. They gather the fuel, but only the Kursh soldiers themselves tend the fire. They are assigned the duty.

"One night a young one fell asleep and the fire died. The others nearly panicked when they awoke to discover the loss! They immediately rekindled the fire and fed it until it towered high and the heat was tremendous. Then the offending soldier, bound hand and foot, was thrown onto the fire. He did not protest. They had planned to attack a small village in the far north—a raid for slaves and goods. After the fire had died they withdrew and returned to their base. It was clear they thought their mission cursed. Is that helpful, Honor?"

"Very much so. I knew that they seldom if ever kept a cold camp, but I had no idea the fire was so important to them. Tsha, that is indeed valuable knowledge. If you felt it necessary to repay my kindness, you have done so."

I waited until dinner was finished to get to the hard questions. I thought they might offer some emotional distress, and I did not want anguish disrupting the meal.

The plates had been cleared and we relaxed with mint tea.

"Tsha, I know that the Aelfir marry young, sometimes as young as fifteen. You have indicated that you were about seventeen when the Kursh took you. You had a husband then?"

She started to protest, then stopped. "Must I answer?"

"I wish you would. You may cry if the telling calls for it."

"Yes, Honor." She kept her eyes focused on the tea cup in her hands. "We had been married barely a year. We had our own small orchard, and a small garden. We had considered having children right away, but Tchon, my husband, thought it best to wait. As you may know, we can prevent conception when we wish.

"There were so many rumors and accounts of the Kursh coming through our lands, killing and burning, that having a child under that threat would not be a blessing."

She stopped for a moment and looked directly at me. "You said before that you are familiar with our troubles."

"Yes. I know that the Kursh have determined to destroy your entire race. They despise the magic that is completely contrary to their nature. This may surprise you, but I and others are working even now to prevent that. We—I—would have the peaceful existence of the Aelfir assured for all time. There may be a way to do that."

"Yes!" Her eyes flashed and I saw for the first time an unguarded display of her emotions. "The Kursh must be destroyed! Kill them all and the Aelfir will be safe! That is what it will take!"

"Yes," I agreed. "We think so too. But please, continue your story."

"Honor? Do you mean that? Do you truly believe that you can end forever the threat of the Kursh?"

"We believe it. In fact, some are certain that it will be so."

"Can I help in some small way? I will do anything to bring that about. I would gladly die if my death brought an end to the terror those creatures visit upon Aelf."

"Perhaps, Tsha, you may indeed contribute to that cause in the future. For now, though, return to your recollection."

"They came, just as the rumors said. They burned our orchard. Four of them came to our house, but we were prepared. We had, of course, no weapons. Tchon killed three of them before they even knew we were in the house. I killed the other. Before we could flee, though, a dozen more arrived. They shot—" here her voice began to tremble. She continued with difficulty, hampered by many pauses and many tears. "—shot Tchon with their arrows from a safe distance. He fell, and died in my arms, his last words of love lost ... in the ... the blood spilling from his lips. So much blood ..." She had to stop there as her throat constricted with tears and speech became impossible.

I waited. Finally she took two ragged breaths and managed to continue.

"They charged, then, to take me prisoner. I had expected that they would kill me, too, but they did not. Two more of them died before I was struck upon the head. When I awoke I was bound hand and foot, and my hands were covered further in a leather bag."

She stopped there, and I did not press her to reveal more. I handed her a lap cloth to wipe her eyes and waited while she composed herself.

"I am sorry, Honor. I did not mean to cry."

"You've done nothing to be sorry for. Tsha, I have one or two more questions. If you were to be allowed free run of the property, garden, house, orchard, and fields, even to the hills on the near horizon, would you attempt to escape?"

She did consider it for a minute before answering. "No, Honor, I would not."

"Why not? Even though you are treated fairly well here, and not beaten, and housed in a clean barracks, still you are a slave. Why would you not try to escape?"

Her voice was ineffably sad as she looked at her hands that still clutched the lap cloth. "My family may all be dead, or scattered, and the land of the Kursh lies between here and there. I have nowhere else to go."

I rose and she did likewise. I walked with her back to the door of the house. Joseph was there with the sentries, lounging and enjoying a discreet amount of beer. They all jumped to attention.

I turned first to Tsha. "I will take you at your word. Trust is a hard thing to earn, and once lost it can never be fully regained."

She replied without hesitation. She stood straight, chin up, eyes meeting mine directly. "I will not lose your trust, Honor. I would not lie to you."

I spoke to Joseph and the sentries. "She is to be allowed free access to all the property. You need not supervise her, or take any responsibility for her movements. She may come and go as a free person, even into the house. But if she is not available when a meal is served, she need not be served another time. And the barracks will be locked as usual. If she is not in them, then she will have to sleep elsewhere. Understood?"

"Yes, Honor," replied the three in unison. Joseph added, "It will be as you say. Shall I have the dress returned to our Matron?"

"No. It is hers now. But I understand that there may be no place in slaves' quarters for her to keep it safely."

I turned back to her. "Change quickly and bring it back to me before you seek your sleep. I will arrange a place for it to be kept for you."

She bowed. "Yes, Honor. Thank you. Thank you many times, and many times over. I shall return quickly."

The other three bowed as well and I went back into the house and closed the door.

She did return quickly, dressed again in slave's garb. I took the dress from her without a word and went directly to my rooms. I left her to take herself back to the barracks. Although that was ungentlemanly treatment of a free woman, it was a sign of trust toward a slave.

The dress had her fragrance upon it. It smelled of leaves and flowers. It did not yet need cleaning. I hung it up in a small hall closet outside my own bedroom that held only the seldom used winter coats.

I lay in bed a long time before sleep came. I was finding it very difficult to proceed as slowly as I felt best. I wanted her in the bed with me. But I was certain that fulfillment of the Prophecy was best served by waiting.

I recalled her words about the Kursh, her obvious hatred of them, and her willingness to sacrifice even her life to destroy them.

That damn Prophecy.

4

THE LOVERS

I FOUND IT DIFFICULT TO MAINTAIN my duties to self and Keep, but I managed. I continued my exercise regimen. Routinely I would ride my horse Roughneck about seven miles out from the Keep (though still on Honor land) and then run back while the horse trotted along beside. He liked occasionally to stop and graze while I ran on ahead, then sprint past me a fair distance, graze again, and wait for me to catch up.

When we returned to the Keep stables we would both be in need of a bath. I would personally wash him down and brush him before turning his care over to the stable master. I continued to devote hours to sparing with sword and spear and even unarmed combat, and of course practice with both the short and long bow. After the running or the exercises I would hurry to the baths before the female members of my family had opportunity to comment on my condition.

I also tended to the duties of the Keep, both as administrator and as commander of the army. I did, however, let my duties to the Brotherhood lapse. Not intentionally; they simply slipped my mind. That alone demonstrated how much my thoughts of Tsha occupied my attention.

I spent more time walking in the garden and orchard after she was given free run of the place. She walked with me most of the time. I felt that a woman of Tsha's history would be better approached with, as Mother had called it, a courtship of sorts. But I found myself enjoying her company. More than that, I looked forward to being with her. The day seemed always a failure until I had seen her and we had shared time together.

She was a woman of clear intelligence and a quietly bold spirit. That spirit had been somewhat cowed by the vicious treatment of the Kursh, but asserted itself again when the fear of abuse disappeared. Her hair had been clipped short by the Kursh as was their preference, and it had been kept so for her work in the shed. Once moved from there, though, she was not required to keep it short and she allowed it to grow past shoulder length. It was gloriously beautiful. My longing for her physically, sexually, was increasing.

The fruit trees were producing like never before. Not only was there more fruit, but the apples, peaches, pears, and grapes were also larger and sweeter. New trees grew straighter and faster from her touch.

We soon had a surplus of fruit—even more than we could sell to the townspeople. I had it distributed fairly among the servants, slaves and the soldiers in the Keep garrison. There was always a healthy supply sent to the main garrison of my troops in Center.

She wandered the fields as well. We had reseeded an area burned by the Kursh months earlier and she spent quite bit of time there. It did not take long for the new plants to catch up to the rest of the crop. Then I told her to cease her magic for a while and report to the Matron.

"Tsha, I know it is against the nature of your people, but I wish you to learn the use of a weapon."

"Master! Honor! For a slave to even touch a weapon is to be put to death!"

"Again, we are not Kursh. True, generally the touch of weapons by a slave is forbidden. But I can ignore those rules when I please. In this Keep, only the Matron and the Maiden—my mother and my sister—would have the authority to object. Neither does. I've already proposed this, and they approve. My sister is just now beginning her lessons with the spear, and having another student at almost the same level will be helpful.

"But you will not be just a sparring partner for her. You will learn, and learn well. My mother is excellent with that weapon, and an excellent teacher.

"You will not be beaten, no matter how poorly you might perform." I grinned. "But if you frustrate the Matron too much, she will unleash upon you a torrent of verbal punishment in a voice so loud that it may leave you wishing for a nice quiet whipping. As it is, you will accumulate a fine set of bruises. Hopefully, you will administer some as well.

"Apply yourself well. I will keep track of your progress. And, Tsha, trust me. I know this is not something you would expect, or even want, but it is a very good idea. Think of it as a skill you will be able to use against the Kursh someday."

She was my guest for dinner every night by then. Mother had tailored a few more dresses and one other pair of sandals. She and Heather had rearranged their own closets to make room for the clothing, and Tsha would enter the house through their entry, change, and come to the dining room. She had at first been very reluctant to take that liberty, but both Mother and Heather reassured her, and insisted. Each told me separately she both liked and respected Tsha and totally approved of her in every respect.

About two weeks later she seemed nervous during the meal; a demeanor that she had mostly conquered recently had returned. I had learned that this was a sign that a significant question was coming. I was not disappointed.

She hesitantly met my eyes. "Master ..."

"'Master?' That means you have a question or a revelation, but fear a reprimand. I would think by now, Tsha, you would have lost that fear."

"I'm sorry, Honor. But barely forty days is not enough to erase the influence of five years of slavery to the Kursh. Besides, I wish to ask something that is truly in the context of slave to master."

I did not reply. Finally she had no choice but to continue.

"Master, I have seen in your eyes that you want me. Yet you have not commanded me to your bed. I must wonder why you do not claim what you own."

"Tsha, as I have said many times, we are not Kursh. Most especially, *I* am not Kursh. I do not own any part of you. I own your labor. You owe me your work, your best efforts, your talents, whatever I might require for the benefit of the Keep. But your body is yours. I am sure you have seen that no slave here is forced to have sex. When one of the Free Peoples—a soldier, a guard, or a guest—wishes for that kind of favor, it is an invitation, not a command, and the slave is free to decline. Some have, and without penalty.

"Tsha, you are unique. Not only because you are Aelfir, though that is certainly much of what makes you special. You were taken into slavery barely an adult. They killed your husband. You were a slave for five years—five years of cruel treatment.

"I have made no secret of my attraction. But I will not command you to that. If anything, because you are special, I accord you at least as much respect as I would—as I have—other slaves. Besides, as the commander of the armies of the Free Peoples as well as Honor of Honor Keep, I must often sacrifice my immediate desires to considerations of what is yet to come."

That was a long speech! Actually, I found it difficult not to tell her more. I was torn between my belief that she deserved to know more and the even stronger belief that events would proceed better if she did not.

She was quiet for many minutes, eyes downcast. Finally, more boldly than before, she looked me in the eyes. "Honor, I will test your patience, and trust to your mercy. I must disagree with you. There is a part of me that you own, that is no longer mine.

"My heart. It is yours now. Now and forever. This slave has fallen in love with her master. Honor, your companion loves you. I have asked why you have not taken me to your bed because I have been hoping that you would."

I had my first surprise of the evening. Not that she loved me. It was, after all, prophesied. It was what I had been hoping for and working toward. The shock was the depth of my own reaction. I had expected to feel simple satisfaction. But no.

I felt joy! My heart thrilled to hear those words! I was in love with Tsha with all my heart and she was in love with me! Nothing could make me happier. I had not realized the depth of my emotions until her confession of her own feelings. I had never expected to feel that kind of love again.

There was no reason to conceal my heart.

I stood up and she, by habit and training, did likewise. There was uncertainty in her expression. I stepped close to her and looked into those big lavender eyes. Then I put my arms around her and kissed her. She froze for a short second, then kissed me back with her entire being, surrendering herself to me without reservation.

After that very long kiss I pulled a bit away and stroked her gorgeous long hair, and caressed her cheek and neck. "Tsha, I have insisted from the beginning that you behave as my equal when we are together. You are my equal now in this matter. If I have your heart, then you have mine. Now and forever. I love you, Tsha." I kissed her again, and she responded again with her whole being.

I scooped her up in my arms. She laughed with unbridled joy, and I echoed her. It was five long strides to the doorway of the dining room, another six strides to the staircase and fifteen steps to the second floor. Then it was another ten strides to my rooms. I carried her the entire distance. We exchanged many kisses during the brief journey, and our laughter echoed through the rooms and halls.

It took too long for us to shed our clothing, anxious as we were, and when we were finally naked together there was no master, no slave, no companion, no Honor. There were just two lovers, our passions evident in our voices and our touches.

Our mutual arousal led, after many long and loving minutes, to ecstatic mutual satisfaction. After I had spent myself, and kissed her many many times, I rolled off her to the side, out of breath.

"But Master," she teased, "surely we aren't done yet."

"Master? Tsha, do not call me that again when we are alone."

"I am sorry, but to address you as 'Honor' seemed somehow inappropriate."

"When we are in private, use my given name."

Her voice became small and apologetic. "I do not know what it is. I have never heard it."

"Oh. It is Collin."

She repeated it once, softly, to test the flavor of it on her tongue.

Then she teased again. "Collin, my love, my lover, surely we are not done?"

"I hope not. But it will take me some minutes to recover."

She laughed. "Oh, I think not. I can help with that."

I got my second surprise of the evening. I discovered that plants were not the only things Tsha could cause to grow, and grow like it had never grown before.

"I must be careful, though," she said, still teasing. "Too much such growth can cause injury."

We pleasured each other for a span that seemed liked hours. And again and again. Every time that I would languish her touch would again bring me back to full virility.

She was never demanding, yet she consumed the sensations of our loving like it was water and she had been weeks in the desert. Nor was it just the physical ecstasies that she craved. It was obvious that she needed the real tenderness of being truly loved. After five years of cruel slavery, abused and assaulted by the Kursh, she was famished for affection, for kisses, for the embrace of true love.

There had been other women in my bed, both slave and free, all there because they wished to be. And some of them—one in particular—had been gloriously responsive, intensely passionate. Yet none had demonstrated the emotions of love and joy that Tsha embodied during our coupling.

Many times while we were joined into a single body, she would clutch tightly, pressing her breasts and belly against me, and rain kisses upon my chest and shoulders and neck and then my lips, shuddering with a joy that could not be only from the physical intimacies we shared. I returned those kisses with equal fervor, and held her tightly, wrapping her in my embrace as completely as my arms could manage.

Many hours later, after my heart and body had settled down and recovered from the unexpected joys and ecstasies, my brain was able to make itself heard. It reminded me that the love and joy I was feeling now would only make it harder and more painful at the end.

Damn Prophecy.

5

THE KURSH

THAT OUR RELATIONSHIP had suddenly changed we neither announced nor hid. That Mother and Heather knew she had finally been to my bed I had no doubt. I thought it likely that the whole Keep was now aware. Daniel certainly knew. Daniel was a boy of fourteen, the son of Joseph and his wife Helen, who was in charge of the Keep's kitchen, kitchen staff, and all things related. She reported to the Matron. Joseph and Helen had both been slaves and had earned their freedom. Daniel was born to them before that, but he was never slave. Honor Keep does not perpetuate slavery across the generations. If a slave woman gives birth, no matter the identity of the father, the child is a free person.

Daniel was a paid servant with one responsibility. He was my messenger, to be always within earshot of my voice while out of sight when possible. He considered the position an enormous honor and privilege and devoted himself to being totally reliable. One part of his requirements was to keep quiet about all he might see or hear when on duty, but I had no delusions about the ability of a boy that age to keep spectacular secrets to himself.

Tsha and I did not behave quite as before. There was more touching, especially of the hands and arms, and she often was bold enough to hang onto my upper arm. We did not exchange kisses publicly. It would not have been proper.

"Tsha, tell me about the death touch. You used it on one of my guards."

She looked around quickly, to assure herself of our privacy. We were in the orchard and there was no one else near. "Collin, the three guards planned to rape me. Or at least the one did, and the others were with him. I protected myself."

"I know. I have no objection to what you did. As you know, Honor Keep does not tolerate rape, no matter the victim. But I want to know how you do what you do. It is important."

She thought for a few minutes, quiet as we strolled among the trees, passing from sunshine to shade and back as the boughs of the trees hid or revealed the sun.

"It is the only weapon the Aelfir have used in generations. It is actually quite simple." She said the next with lowered voice, conspiratorially. "As you have experienced, we can make living things grow, and it is not restricted to plants." She then continued with her voice at normal volume. "We touch the forehead, just as we touch trees and stems, and will the sudden uncontrolled growth of the brain. It takes only a very little growth to rupture blood vessels, and death results."

"I suspected something of the sort. But how do you learn such a thing in the first place, or become proficient?"

"Children are required to practice from the earliest age that they can demonstrate their heritage. And we practice often even into adulthood, trying to get faster and more efficient."

"Practice? I would think you'd run out of practice subjects very quickly."

"We can practice on the dead, but that is not the usual method. Too difficult to see results of the attempt."

She looked quickly around and then plucked an apple from a nearby branch. She handed it to me like a prize. "The art is to cause the growth of something that you cannot see, but you know is there. This apple has small seeds in the core. I cannot see them, or know exactly their location inside the apple. But I can still cause one to grow."

She opened my fingers so the apple rested on my palm. Then she put her hand on the apple and stared at it for only a few seconds. My gut shivered as I felt the apple twitch on its own.

"Please open it."

I took my knife from my belt and sliced the apple in half. It was obvious. One of the seeds had actually sprouted a tiny green sprig within the apple.

She smiled triumphantly. "You can imagine what such a sudden burst of growth to the brain would do."

"I'm impressed. I'm glad I've witnessed it, but as I said, I suspected the method. I have given some thought to this, Tsha. Tell me, must it be your hand that touches? Could you cause the growth with, say, a foot? Or a knee? Or perhaps your lips?"

She chuckled and spoke softly. "My lover knows from experience that I can produce healthy growth with my lips."

I chuckled also. "Yes. But can you cause," I indicated the apple "this kind of unhealthy growth?"

She frowned, thinking, remembering. "I do not know. We have always been taught to use the hands, the fingers, where touch is most sensitive."

"Your lips are quite sensitive, too, Tsha. That also I know from experience."

At that point we both heard the approach of hurrying footsteps. A moment later Daniel appeared from around a bend in the path. He was not quite out of breath, but clearly he had trotted from the entrance to the orchard that was closest to the house, and our wanderings had taken us nearly a mile from that point.

He bowed. "Honor, the western garrison has sent a message. There are two wagons that seek admittance. They are traders. Kursh traders."

I responded almost at once. "Daniel, tell them to message back to let them wait. I'll give them further instructions when I get to the house garrison. Then run to the Matron and request an outdoor cloak and hood for Tsha and bring it back to us. We'll be walking back to the gate."

Daniel bowed and hurried back the way he'd come. When he was out of sight I took Tsha by the hand and led her behind some foliage where we would be completely unobserved from any direction.

Our discussion had aroused me. I wanted to have her right then. But I settled for less. I kissed her and as always she kissed back with all of herself, pressing against me and surrendering herself to me, promising unending love to me in that kiss.

"I do not want any Kursh to have even a chance to observe your presence. When Daniel brings back the cloak, put it on and do not forget the hood. Conceal yourself so that you might be any free woman of any station strolling through the orchard. And do stroll! Do not act like you are hiding or that you do not belong. You may go up with Mother and Heather and observe with them when the traders arrive. You were with the Kursh for five years. You may hear or see something that may be of use. But you must wear the cloak and hood. Tell my mother I suggested they do the same, so that you blend in and do not appear different."

She bowed, smiling. "Yes, Honor. It will be as you say."

I grinned back. "I must hurry. You must not." Then I gave her another quick kiss and jogged along the path toward the gate. When I met Daniel, I told him that after he had delivered the clothing to Tsha he should hurry back to the house and wait there with the ladies. I would have no messages for him to deliver, but they might.

He bowed. "Yes, Honor. It will be as you say."

"Well done, Daniel. Thank you." I set out at a jog to the gate, Daniel grinning proudly behind me.

I skirted the house and went directly to the garrison a few hundred yards to the north. I did not take time to acknowledge the hurried bows, but sprinted up the stairs to the signal area on the roof.

The captain (of the guard) greeted me. "Honor! Thank you for the visit!"

I returned his bow. "Captain, it is my privilege to visit. I regret that I do not do so more often. What more do we know of our visitors?"

"There are two wagons, Honor, and they are Kursh. They claim to be traders. Our men at the border count seven men total."

"Armed?"

"Swords, knives, longbows. What would be normally expected."

"How about merchandise? Do they carry a suitable variety of trade goods to make the visit worthwhile?"

"Ah! That, Honor, had not been asked."

He looked to the signalman. "Send the question."

The signal man turned to face the western garrison. He used a hand-held mirror and reflected the sunlight in coded flashes seen by signalmen in the other garrison.

The wait was several minutes for the answer: "Yes."

"Signal them to escort the traders to the staging area west of the house. Send our own escort to meet them so they can return."

"Honor, with all due respect, is that the wisest course? Might we not be better off to send them on their way?"

I could not help but smile. Halyar was sometimes too cautious. He was about my mother's age, and had been my father's second in command for many years. He still, I think, blamed himself for Father's death, even though there was absolutely no reason for that. But both my parents had been good friends with him even before I was born and he took my welfare quite personally.

"Captain, you are correct. It is not the wisest course at all. But in this case, I believe it is the necessary one. For the long term."

"Oh. Because of the ... ?"

"Yes, Captain. Because of that. I will meet them myself at the staging area, as will you and six men. See to it that a suitable guard of archers is placed high as well. Just in case."

"Yes, Honor. It will be as you say. Thank you for the visit."

Appearances are important. To have me standing at the designated area, awaiting their arrival, would give them an impression of importance that they did not rate. Conversely, my not meeting them at all would send a message of trust and acceptance that would be blatantly false, even to them.

So, when they arrived at the staging area—a fenced-in area between the house and the garrison—they found Captain Halyar waiting for them while I arrived from around a corner of the house, neither hurrying nor dawdling, but keeping the correct pace for a man of my station attending to business.

Halyar had halted the wagons just outside the gate to the enclosure. When he saw me walking toward him he instructed the traders to leave the wagons and stand next to them, and for their leader to walk alone into the enclosure.

I watched this closely. You can tell a lot about a man by how he dismounts from a wagon and how he walks. I saw that he wore his sword on his right side. I did not doubt that he was effective with that weapon. A left-handed swordsman always has a slight advantage over right-handers because we seldom encounter them while they are accustomed to fighting against right-handers.

The Kursh sword is about two feet long, the blade is flat and straight, both sides edged, tapering suddenly to a point. It is a strong weapon made for a crowded battlefield or a one-on-one duel.

The Free Peoples' soldiers generally use a slightly longer and leaner saber. The blade is sharp all the way to the guard on one side and about half-way down the other, the blade having just a slight curve. On the battle field there is no clear advantage to either weapon. But in a duel the saber is slightly superior because of its greater length.

I was not wearing my own sword. I do not wear it in the Keep, unless I am expecting violence, and sometimes not even then.

I noticed also that four men exited the back wagon, while two plus the leader had exited from the front one. They were all typical Kursh—about the same in height and build as my own people, but swarthy, with shiny black hair and dark eyes and sharp bony noses above thin lips. All the men were clean-shaven, which was unusual for traders, though not unheard of. However, they did all wear brightly colored tunics of red, blue, and yellow. That was typical.

Both wagons were about twelve feet long by eight wide and near to eight feet from ground to top. All four sides were concealed by dark hanging cloth. These were standard for an overland trader, whether Kursh or otherwise. I did, mostly by the luck of a breeze, note that a hole existed in the front cloth of the first wagon. That was not standard, but could simply be blamed on a recent mishap.

The leader approached me, stopped at the distance showing respect and peaceful intentions and bowed. I did not, of course, return the bow.

"I am Honor of Honor Keep. Welcome, Trader. I hope the land and weather have been beneficial to you."

"Thank you for the greeting, Honor of Honor Keep. I am Dort, trader. The weather and land have been, if not beneficial, at least not turned against us. We might still see a profit on this trip. Shall we display our wares?"

He looked up at the balconies, where at least a dozen women, every one of them cloaked and hooded (Mother, thank you!) watched and listened to the exchange. Above them, the archers stood on the roof, bows half-drawn and ready.

"We have quite an inventory of jewelry, combs and brushes, cloth and clothing, sandals, and hats and scarves. Plus, of course, boots, scabbards, smith's tools, and other goods of interest to men."

"Perhaps in a moment. Tell me, Dort, what direction do you come from, and where do you intend to go when finished here?"

As we spoke, we were doing a little dance although he was not aware of it as such. When I had presented myself to him I had been careful to put him between myself and the front wagon. As he spoke, he had tried to move himself unobtrusively out of that line, and I had very firmly moved with him to keep him in that line.

"In your lands, we have been in the west, from the north to the south. We expect to go to our homeland from here and hopefully trade what we have for gold and silver. There is always a good demand for the goods from your lands in Kursh. We hope, even to acquire a slave or two to take with us."

"Really? Any particular type? Males? Females? Any particular skills or traits?"

His eyes narrowed. I had given him the opening he had hoped for.

"Actually, yes. We have heard that there is a female slave here—an Aelfir. We were hoping to acquire her. The demand for such is exceptionally high in Kursh and we would be certain to turn a profit."

"Really? Your sources are out of date. Such a slave was here, working on the reaping floor. Her production was terrible and I sold her to Fair Keep for a dancer from the far north."

He hesitated, and his eyes seemed to look past me to something or someone at my back. Anger flashed for an instant, and then faded. He spoke as one inventing an unexpected story. "Honor, those at Fair Keep knew nothing of such a slave."

"When was that, Dort? You said you have been in the west, but Fair Keep is northeast of here."

He made no attempt to hide his anger this time. He spoke harshly, almost snarling.

"We know that she is here! We are willing to pay the highest price! Our entire inventory is yours for this one slave."

"I do believe you will pay the highest price, but you will get no slave. We have too much respect for our female slaves to sell them to a gang of *Cherromarcols* (this was a Kursh word meaning, approximately, those who have sex with homosexual dogs. It was their worst possible insult).

His face got suddenly darker and his left hand went to his sword hilt and began to draw his blade. At his first move I stepped forward and put my left hand across his, preventing him from drawing the blade. He strained briefly to overpower me, but could not.

He then became aware that my right hand had put the point of my knife delicately to his throat.

"You would draw your sword against me? If I had not stopped you, you would have enough arrows in you to fill a quiver." I spoke quietly. No one but he could hear my words.

"Would you die so easily without even coming close to fulfilling your objective?"

He strained once more, suddenly, in an attempt to draw his blade. It moved a few inches before I again exerted enough force to push the blade down completely into the scabbard. He snarled.

"What objective do you think you mean, hair-faced late-comer? Too busy to shave these last weeks?"

"I prefer to wear the beard as it emphasizes the difference between me and you Kursh frog slime."

He turned even redder and strained again to draw his weapon, without success.

"Your objective is the acquisition of the slave and my death. You came here charged with the duty of accomplishing at least one of those two deeds.

"I will say that I appreciate your courage. You and your men are willing to die right here if you can bring about my death. Well, I suspect you will die right here, whether you accomplish your objective or not."

He made a real effort to move to the side again, or even to turn me so that I was exposed to the front of the wagon, but I did not allow it.

I turned to Halyar. "Captain, there is one more Kursh in the front wagon. He has a crossbow. Drag him out of there and no need to be gentle."

"Sir!" responded Halyar and gave orders immediately to a few men to accomplish the deed.

Dort's eyes grew wide. "How did you know? What kind of magic do you command?"

"Release your grip on your sword and let your hand fall to the side." We locked eyes for a moment. He tried once more to pull the sword free, without success. I pushed the point of my knife barely into the soft flesh of his throat. He glared, but then defiantly did as he was told.

"You cow turds have been trying to kill me since I was ten years old. Don't you suppose I've learned a little in fifteen years? That you were assassins I knew the minute you dismounted from the wagon and walked toward me. You are clearly an officer in the Kursh army, and your men are soldiers.

"I saw the hole in the front cloth of the wagon. Your pitiful attempt to put me in the line of fire was also a clear revelation that an archer hid within the first wagon. It must be a crossbow because there is no room there to draw a long bow.

"You keep trying to foil your prophecy. When will you learn that it is just that—prophecy? It will happen. Every time that you try to defeat it, it turns out badly for you. We have learned that lesson the hard way, but at least we have learned it."

I stepped away and withdrew my blade from his throat. I noticed that at least two archers still had him targeted. They had relaxed their bows, but would be able to shoot him long before he would be able to reach me with his sword.

I looked past him at the wagon and he turned to do likewise. Soldiers roughly dragged a Kursh from the wagon and cast him to the ground. Another soldier emerged from the wagon carrying a cocked and loaded crossbow.

Halyar looked at me. "A demonstration, Honor?"

I nodded. Halyar tore a piece of crimson cloth from the soldier's tunic and tied it to the bolt on the crossbow, just behind the tip. He then looked upward to his archers.

"Allen! On the way up. Hanna, on the way down."

He motioned the soldier that held the crossbow, and he fired the bolt up and away from the archers. As it reached the level of the roof and rose above it an arrow sang through the air and pierced the cloth. That disrupted the flight path of the bolt and it faltered, waivered, and then turned awkwardly and fell back to earth. As it did so a second arrow whipped through the air and skewered the crimson.

There was applause from the other soldiers, the women on the balconies, and the many civilians that had arrived to trade with the newcomers.

I turned to Dort. "That is why we will win. Not because of any prophecy, not because of anything I or that Aelfir slave will do. We will win because our warriors are more skilled than yours."

He glared at me again. "Not with swords! Not with spears or axes! In those we are superior. If you have courage, let us fight for our lives with those weapons."

I glanced quickly at Halyar, who nodded.

"Very well, Dort. And since you are the commander of this small group, I take it that you are the most skillful?"

"I am!"

"Then you will get your first chance, plus your opportunity to fulfill your assignment." I turned to one of the house servants that stood behind me. I was not surprised that it was Trig. Most of the household, servants and slaves as well as family, had turned out to see the traders.

"Trig, go to my room and fetch my sword and scabbard. Not the ornate one of a commander, but the plain one for battle."

"Yes, Honor! As you say!" He ran into the house.

I spoke again to the Kursh leader. "I am feeling especially generous. If you manage to kill me, you will be allowed to leave here alive and report that your mission was a success."

I turned to Halyar. "Captain, that is a true offer. If he wins he has earned the right to live."

Halyar grinned and chuckled. "Yes, Honor. It will be as you say." And he stifled another grin.

"Treachery! He laughs because you lie! If I kill you I will be tortured and put to death! You would never let me leave here!"

"Captain, tell the Kursh exactly why you are amused."

Halyar faced the Kursh. "I am amused because I have seen my commander use his sword. You have no chance."

The Kursh glared at him. "You have not seen me use mine!"

Halyar shrugged. "It would make no difference."

Trig returned with the sword. I examined the weapon carefully but quickly, then buckled the belt around my waist and adjusted it while I spoke to Dort.

"All of your men will have the opportunity to fight for their lives. I know this is something that you or your countrymen would never offer in sincerity, but we, proudly, are not Kursh. Of course, chances are that you will not live to see if any of them are successful, but you can go to your grave knowing they had the same chance you received."

I was ready. I stood before him. "Officer Dort, you may draw your weapon and attack."

His hand flashed to the hilt of his sword and drew it, thinking, perhaps, to get to me before I had cleared my blade. He was disappointed. But attack he did, with all the skill and ferocity he could muster.

After the first exchange I knew that he was out-matched. After the second exchange, so did he. I could have ended it quickly, but it had been a while since I'd had a real workout with the weapon. I dueled defensively only, not attacking or even counter-attacking, but simply parrying or avoiding his thrusts and slashes. I was aware, of course, that everyone was watching us, including my mother, sister, and Tsha. I'll admit I was showing off a little.

He was getting frustrated. He was skilled enough to know that I could have killed him several times and had simply declined the opportunity. He increased the furious pace of his attack, employing every trick he knew to even draw blood.

As we turned and moved in the make-shift arena I noticed Daniel standing next to Trig. He would not be there unless he had a message for me.

While I continued to parry, I held up my left hand. "Stop! There is other business I must attend. Withdraw for a moment and regain your breath."

He ignored me and continued his attack, slashing at my face, lunging the point of his sword at my belly, even trying to slash my thighs or arms.

"I said to stop for a moment!"

He growled a reply, "If you wish to stop, surrender. Otherwise I will continue until one of us is dead!" And he again tried to take my life.

"That is enough." I quickly went on the offensive and after a flurry of moves I disarmed him. His sword flew from his fingers and landed on the ground. I went to it and picked it up, holding it by the grip in my left hand. I scowled at him. "Now just wait! We will finish this in a moment. Besides, you look like you could use a rest."

I then turned my back on him and walked over to Daniel. His labored breathing made it easy to hear that he followed though not too closely.

I must admit here that when I deal with the Kursh it often feels like cheating. I seem to know what they are going to do even before they know themselves. While I received Daniel's message I stood facing sideways to Dort, my left side nearest, unobtrusively keeping one eye on him while giving Daniel the attention of my ears.

Without the slightest warning the Kursh drew his knife and charged, knife in the air, intending to stab downward at my neck.

I raised my left hand and he ran himself onto his own sword.

His charge had enough force to push my elbow close to my body and he got close enough to stab downward. But even as the blade pierced him my right hand came up with my sabre and across my body and upward in defense. The sharp edge stopped his wrist. Though it did not chop through the bones, it did sever the tendons that allowed him to grip, along with the artery that runs to the thumb. The fingers went slack, the knife fell to the ground, and he did likewise a moment later, his last breath spraying blood into the air as he died. I had pushed him away as I loosed my grip on his sword and he finished on his back, the weapon sticking upward from his belly like a monument erected upon a small hill.

I turned my full attention to Daniel. I was aware of the buzzing of the crowd, and the light applause from my household and soldiers, but I did not acknowledge it. That would have been frivolous.

"Are you certain?"

He nodded vigorously, eyes still wide from what he had just witnessed. That was his first close acquaintance with violent death.

I looked up at the balconies and caught my mother's eye. She nodded firmly. I motioned my agreement. She and the two women standing with her disappeared from the balcony.

His wrist and belly had poured quite a lot of blood upon me. I would need water and soap to get clean, plus of course a change of clothing. I wiped the blood from my forehead with my left hand, and then the blood from my blade on his shirt and returned it to the scabbard.

"Captain, get a couple of Kursh and have them toss this body beside one of the wagons."

"Yes Sir! And a pleasure to see your skills at work again."

I bowed shortly. "Thank you Captain. After you've taken care of that, choose four of your men to duel four of theirs. The last three are already spoken for."

He looked suddenly very stern. "May I choose myself, Honor?"

"Choose whoever you wish. But save your own duel for last."

"Yes, Honor, it will be as you say. Sergeant! Bring four of the—" he hesitated a second, then emphasized the next word, "—prisoners into the enclosure along with yourself, the corporal, and Franklin."

This order was quickly carried out. None of the Kursh had been disarmed, so all still had their swords.

"Captain, not that one," I commanded, indicating the Kursh that had hidden in the wagon with the crossbow. "He will defend himself later."

Halyar had him taken out of the enclosure and another took his place.

I asked one of them, "Do you wish your fight for your lives to be one-on-one four times, or four-on-four?"

He caught the eyes of the three and they all agreed. One-on-one. So the townspeople (by now standing two and three deep around the enclosure) and household were witness to four duels.

I did not intend it as a spectacle for their entertainment. It was literally a fight for life. I would have preferred private duels. But there was no way to do that with the gathered crowd.

I watched each match carefully, noting the strengths and weaknesses of my own men. They all did very well. I noticed also that every single one of the Kursh used the same technique. The same teacher had trained them all. A teacher who's technique had a weakness against a feint-and-shift to the right.

During the second match I was joined at the gate closest to the house by three women, cloaked and hooded. One of them spoke to me immediately.

"Honor, I feared for you. I have seen that man before, and I knew he was skilled. I had no idea your skills were so superior."

"It is required," I answered. "How could I expect my men to trust me and follow me and pledge their lives to me if I could not do at least as well as they on the field?"

"Actually, Tsha, Collin is modest. There may not be a better swordsman among the Free Peoples."

"Thank you, Mother. And my compliments for your initiative on dressing all the ladies the same. An excellent way to keep our young Aelfir woman anonymous. Although it seems right now that the precaution will prove unnecessary." As I said that, the second match ended with the Kursh soldier dead at the feet of the corporal.

The sergeant and the captain made short and merciful work of their opponents. Three Kursh remained.

"Mother, you are certain of this? You have not seen them use a spear. They may be more skilled with that weapon than with swords."

"Collin, you are not the only expert in weaponry in this family. It is obvious they were all trained by the same barely competent teacher. They all move like their feet are trapped in mud. Not only do I need the practice, but my two students are ready for a live test. They must get one sometime, and when better?"

"Very well. I trust your judgment." I drew Heather off to the side while Mother did some last-minute coaching with Tsha. "Heather, Mother and Tsha are protected somewhat by the prophecy. They may be wounded, but we know they will not be killed. But the prophecy mentions you not at all. You are in the most danger."

"I know that, Collin. I am not afraid. As Mother said, it is time. Time also for me to do my share in the family destiny. Time to baptize my weapon in Kursh blood."

I had to grin. "Spoken like a true warrior of the Keep. Now fight like one. Keep your focus and remember your lessons. Let your body act and react as it has been taught."

The three remaining prisoners were ushered into the enclosure. They were required to exchange their swords for spears. Any male soldier worth his salt, whether of the Free Peoples or of the Kursh, is trained in the bow, the spear, and the sword. Female soldiers seldom receive training in the sword; with that weapon they can be overmatched simply by sheer strength. But with the spear, the distance between combatants nullifies much of the strength advantage and favors quickness and coordination—traits women can have in equal measure to men.

In combat like this, of course, the spear would never be thrown. If the thrower missed his target, he was defenseless. Also, these spears were not built to be thrown with any accuracy. I had seen them thrown in battle on occasion, but only when another spear or sword was immediately available to the thrower. That would not be the case here.

Mother had decided to take the first match herself, and had indicated firmly that her opponent be the one that had part of his crimson shirt missing. She removed her cloak and hood and stepped forward.

The Kursh grinned. A woman. And one old enough, perhaps, to be his mother. This would not be so difficult after all. I suspect he felt that he might actually get out of this alive.

But to his credit he was cautious. Mother did nothing but defend on the first two exchanges, parrying his thrusts and making him work his feet. She was right. His footwork was terrible. He didn't lift his feet and twice he almost stumbled when forced to move sideways quickly. And this was on smooth hard ground. If he had to fight on rough terrain, or a battlefield with bodies and weapons strewn about, and muddy spots caused by blood, a skilled opponent would finish him quickly.

His handwork, however, was quite good and he taxed Mother very well over the first few minutes. I heard Tsha and Heather talking to each other, pointing out what to watch out for and what might give them an advantage.

Apparently Mother decided after several minutes that her pupils had seen enough. She had seen the same weakness I had. She used a feint-and-shift to the right, then the left, and then the right again. The Kursh tangled up his own feet and almost fell before he was skewered neatly through the chest. His body was hauled away and tossed on the pile with the others.

Heather removed her cloak and hood and stepped forward, Mother's last bit of advice fresh in her mind. That advice was to not show off, not hesitate, and finish him as quickly and as safely as possible.

The Kursh next in line also strode to the center of the make-shift arena. He looked at Heather, then at Mother, and then at me. He saw Heather's sharp gray eyes and long reddish-brown hair, now constrained in a simple tie behind her head, and the structure of her nose and chin. He recognized that she was almost certainly my sister, and the daughter of the woman that had bested his companion. He noted, too that she was young, probably still short of full maturity.

I'm guessing too that he noticed she was beautiful. Sometimes a Kursh male would be hesitant to kill a young and beautiful woman. He would rather take her prisoner and enslave her, to use later.

But this one hesitated not a second. He advanced against her quickly, moving the spear head forward in feints and half-thrusts, forcing Heather to retreat and possibly leave an opening. She appeared to stumble, and he charged in quickly to finish her. The stumble had been, of course, faked, and her spear point, seemingly totally out of position, was whipped back immediately to the front and the charging Kursh was stopped as the spear point pierced his belly just below the breastbone. Heather gripped the spear shaft harder and thrust the point in deeper, forcing the man backward and finally on his back. When he gurgled his last breath and the blood poured from his open mouth, and his fingers had released his spear, then Heather put her foot on his body and withdrew the weapon.

She turned away from him and walked back to us, a grim look on her face I'd never seen before. Appropriately, she did not acknowledge the scattered applause.

"Well done, Sister! You have made me proud!"

"I as well am proud of you," Mother added. "An excellent reaction to his aggression."

Heather's grim look faded, replaced by a big smile. She turned and watched the body of her enemy get dragged out of the enclosure and tossed atop the others.

It was Tsha's turn. She was not yet comfortable with the spear.

Heather had grown up seeing her parents and brother, and others, practicing with the weapon and using it. Though her lessons had not gone on long, she had held the weapon in her hands often through the years, and had carried one or more even as a little girl. She had a relaxed familiarity with the weapon.

Not so Tsha. She had seen the things used in battle a few times while enslaved by the Kursh, but had never touched one before her lessons started here. The Aelfir did not use weapons yet when she was taken. They were at this time beginning to learn to use the bow and the spear, but she did not know that and it would have made no difference in her adjustment.

The use of a weapon for killing another was against her nature. She would use the death touch to protect herself, but killing another simply because he was an enemy, or as a task set before her, was not a thing she had as yet reconciled to herself.

When she removed her cloak and hood, the remaining Kursh looked at first quite surprised, and then pleased. He recognized the woman as the slave they were meant to acquire. Killing her would be considered a success. Too, since she was Aelfir, she would not be skilled with a weapon.

Tsha took her stance well and fought him evenly for several minutes. But after he had tested her, he changed his tactics. He went into defensive mode and allowed her to attack. He retreated before her, pretending to think himself overmatched. An experienced and confident fighter would have recognized this tactic, but Tsha did not.

Eventually she over-extended a thrust and he was able to side-step and actually grabbed her spear behind the point and pulled it from her grasp. He tossed it away. There was a gasp of concern from the audience, and even from Mother and Heather. Tsha looked frightened—paralyzed with fear and surprise.

The Kursh grinned with triumph, stepped forward confidently and much too casually thrust the point of his spear directly at her belly.

Tsha turned to the side and the point missed her by inches only. Then she grabbed the shaft of his spear and pulled herself toward him. She put her other hand quickly on his forehead. She held that position for only a few seconds and the man fell at her feet and lay dead, facing the sky.

She stood over him, then turned, walked over to her spear, picked it up, and walked back to us. She did not look triumphant. Much like Heather, she looked grim. She came and stood before me, close, and looked at me.

I folded my arms and looked at her sternly, which she obviously did not expect. She looked confused, apprehensive.

"Tsha, you are not done. You must go back and put the point of your spear into his body. You must pierce his heart or impale him in the center of his belly."

"But, Honor, he is dead."

"No matter. You used your spear, and your enemy is dead. You must blood your weapon. How can you trust your weapon in the future if it cannot trust you to use it well?"

"Is that not a mere superstition?"

"Is it? Most people believe that the death touch is mere superstition. Even some of those here that just witnessed it will not believe how he died.

"Tsha, superstition or not, do this thing." I then went to her and spoke softly, so that only she could hear. "Tsha, I love you. I would not insist on this if it was not important. But I do insist. Trust me. Besides, he is Kursh. Think of Tchon, and your years of slavery."

I stepped away from her. She looked at me with sad eyes, but then turned and did as instructed. She poised herself over the body. She set her feet, then took her spear, raised her hands high, and drove the point downward into his chest. I witnessed a change in her right then. She pulled the point out, then stabbed downward again, and then again, surrendering to a sudden rage that kept her thrusting the spear point into the body a dozen times, each time with more force than the one before.

Her audience had given mild applause after the first stroke, knowing the tradition of blooding the weapon. But then as her assault went on, a shocked or uneasy silence was their only reaction.

I was nearly as shocked as they, but not displeased. A battle rage that was foreign to her nature—to the nature of all Aelfir— had been awakened. It might be very useful later.

I did not stop her, despite the curious looks from Mother and Heather. I allowed fatigue to end the assault.

Finally spent, breathing ragged, arms atremble, she turned away from the body and walked back to me. No longer was her gait or manner submissive. It was almost defiant. She stood before me, breathing hard, eyes flashing ice.

Her face, arms, hands, feet and clothing were splattered with blood.

"Honor, I trust that was sufficient." Her tone, though, said that it might be a long time before she forgave me.

"Yes it was. Well done." Then I laughed shortly. "You are in need of a bath even more than I!" I dismissed propriety for a moment and took her in my arms. I gave a quick kiss on the cheek and spoke quietly.

"It really was necessary, Tsha. I intend to send the bodies back to Kursh. They must not see that one of them was killed with no outward wound. They would know an Aelfir had done it. They suspect that you are here. We cannot allow them to be certain."

After a minute I held her away from me. Heather and Mother then embraced her and told her she had done well.

I motioned Mother to come with me and the two of us walked over to Halyar. "Captain, have their goods removed from their wagon. Mother, would be so kind as to see to the distribution? Whatever you see fit? Tsha will help you if you wish."

"Yes, she and Heather and the entire house staff can help. Can it wait until we clean up a little?"

I looked pointedly at the crowd of townspeople gathered around. They had all come, originally, to do business with the traders.

"What do you think?"

She looked at the crowd and sighed. "I'll use some of the Captain's troops to keep order." She looked at me with a twinkle in her eye. "And what will you be doing while we are hard at work? Bathing, I suppose?"

"Unfortunately, no. I want my favorite slave to help me with that, especially as she will need the bath as much as I. Since she'll be assisting you, I guess that will have to wait. I do have other business to take care of."

I walked over to the wagons and waited until all the goods had been taken from them and set upon the ground inside the compound. Halyar had set a few of his men to keep the townspeople outside of the compound and orderly. Mother and her assistants immediately assumed command of the distribution. This was a windfall for the townspeople as well as many from the Keep. I suspected that Mother would give away everything based on need.

I went inside the wagons and looked around. There was nothing there of any use. I did, mostly out of curiosity, examine the hole in the front flap of the first wagon. It was perfectly placed to allow a crossbow marksman to fire through it at a designated target.

"Captain," I said as I climbed out, "toss the bodies into the two wagons. Have them driven near the Kursh border, and then set the horses to continue into that land. I'm sure the smell will attract someone after they cross the border. Let Turg see what comes of his attempts to foil prophecy. Then I think the Matron may have other duties for you to attend to."

"Yes, Honor. It will be as you say."

Halyar assigned his soldiers to their tasks and it was not very many minutes later that the two wagons were on their way east accompanied by a half dozen warriors and two riderless mounts.

I stood to the side and watched Mother organize the distribution. She was efficient, pleasant, barely compromising, and treated the slaves and servants as respected employees. She had indicated to me with a few subtle looks that she wished to talk privately.

She set the perimeters of her preferences, then left the actual distribution to Heather, Helen, and the staff. She stepped over to the gate and talked to Halyar. As she turned away and came toward me, I saw Halyar reorganizing the lines of citizens from the town. The poorest were invited to the front and those more well-to-do were directed to the back. Some of these, grumbling, walked or rode back to town.

"Collin, how did you know they were not legitimate traders?"

"Having no beards was suspicious, but when Dort came off the wagon and walked to me I knew he was an officer in their army. Didn't you?"

"No. I'll plead the excuse that my angle of view was not as good as yours. But it was clear even before that that you suspected them. Can you tell me why?"

"Halyar spoke to you about my visit to the garrison. He shares too much with you. The prophecy, Mother. I know you've paid little attention to the details, and I understand why. But, although I curse the thing regularly, it is sometimes useful.

"You know, of course, that Tsha and I have professed our love."

"Indeed. The two of you were loud enough when you carried her to your rooms. You've made no secret of the fact. Yet, Collin, I must say that I appreciate the way you've maintained propriety. She is still a slave."

"For a while yet. Back to the prophecy. As I said, it is sometimes useful. It has these lines:

Their love declared,
Failed assassins dead,
The slave from Aelf he frees himself
The day of eight with the Brothers shared
And on that day the two are wed.

"I don't care much for that third line. The rhyme isn't very good. But since Tsha and I did declare our love to each other, I've been expecting would-be assassins. When the Kursh wagons arrived at our western border, it seemed only logical.

"Oh, I had not said so before, but it was very good to see you with a spear again. You've forgotten nothing and you don't seem to have slowed down."

"Or at least not much, eh? Thank you, it was good to get back into warrior work for a time.

"So when do you anticipate freeing your slave? Obviously before the observance of your title day."

"I don't know. I think I might do it that same day, though I will tell her earlier. Free her and then marry her. Two things to celebrate and one to both celebrate and mourn."

"Your ascent to the title, and your father's death. There will be others to mourn his death as well."

"Yes. Some still do almost every day just as we do. Halyar does, as you know. So does Captain Krushek. So do those that knew him well and served him. The other Keeps will be here, and you know Richard grieves as deeply as we."

I looked at the activity. The piles of trade goods had dwindled to almost nothing. There was one pile set off to the side. That was for the servants and slaves to pick from.

"Mother, if you are done with my slave, might I have her back? We both need to bathe."

"I suppose so. Collin, don't you think you should tell her?"

"No. I want to, but I think I will not."

"Why not?"

"Mother, we do so many things because of that damn prophecy. I especially. I allowed the Kursh here because the prophecy had foretold their coming. It foretold her coming, and I brought her in the house and, to use your term, courted her because the prophecy had foretold our love. It has become self-fulfilling. I want all of her actions, and her decisions, to be what is in her heart without knowledge of what is supposed to be. She will make her own decisions without influence of the prophecy. At the worst it will make no difference. And telling her might well steal from her—from us—the happiness we share right now."

She nodded. "All right, Collin. I should have known you'd have good reason. You are your father's son, after all. I will tell Heather not to mention it.

"Now," she tossed aside the somber mood and teased, "who shall we ladies choose to help us bathe?"

"Whoever you want. You could get Halyar to help you. It would not be the first time."

"Collin! How dare you suggest such a thing?"

I laughed. "Lady Elizabeth, what kind of a commander would I be if I did not know how my second in command spends his off-duty hours?"

"Oh, so you are spying on him, and not me."

"I would never spy on you, Mother. I'm not prepared to be that thoroughly shocked at what I might find out."

We both laughed. Then she walked to where Heather and the rest were finishing up. She took Tsha over to the reserved pile and invited her to take anything she liked.

Tsha, after hesitation, picked out a silver bracelet with violet stones. It looked to me to be a valuable piece. It would look good on her even when she wore naught else, but would complement that first dress she wore wonderfully. She tried it on, looked quite pleased, and walked to me. She bowed.

"Master, I am told you have a duty for me."

"You are told correctly." I dropped my voice. "And I will allow you that use of 'Master' because we are in public. It is appropriate, and will be so in the bath, since staff will be around. But I had better not hear it tonight."

She smiled sunshine. Apparently, I was forgiven. I walked then to the house and to the bath facilities in the back. She followed a step behind, as a slave should.

6

ᴛ̄ʜᴇ ꜰʀɪᴇɴᴅ

TSHA AND I HAD AN EXCELLENT BATH. We both made sure the other was quite clean. With staff in attendance, supplying hot water, soap, towels, and so on, we did nothing more than help each other wash.

The bath chamber is the Keep's most specific nod to luxury. It is in the back of the house, with two private stairways, one leading to my rooms, the other leading to Mother's and Heather's. The guest quarters are a building attached to the house, with its own entrance to the chamber. There is also a door to the outside where a huge metal vessel sits above a fire and water is heated for the baths. Slaves or servants carry the hot water into the tubs. Cold water is added directly with pipes that run from the wells.

It is a large room, with four separate tubs. Each tub is wooden, watertight of course, about six feet wide by four feet deep—enough room for three or four people if necessary, but quite roomy for two. Three feet of the depth is below the wooden floor, and of course there are small steps inside. A simple plug in a wall near the bottom allows drainage.

Heather came in perhaps ten minutes after we got there. She was accompanied by Fia, her personal attendant. Fia was a slave given to Heather by Lars as a present on her sixteenth naming day celebration. She'd been freed from a Kursh company of soldiers in what Lars liked to call a "liberation raid." He and his men liberated some land, animals, and property from a Kursh encampment established on the wrong side of the border.

Fia had been in the hands of the Kursh for three years after they killed her parents in a raid on a Northland village. She was about thirteen years old, and absolutely devoted to Heather.

I was surprised that Mother had not come down. I suspected then that she had indeed planned on bathing with Halyar but did not wish to share that pairing with her children. I found it amusing, but at the same time regretful that I had teased her into deciding to delay her bath.

As we were drying ourselves, and each other, Daniel appeared.

He bowed. "Honor, we have visitors." He glanced slyly at my sister and lowered his voice. "It is Fair and his guard."

"Huh! Busy day! Daniel, tell Fair where you found me. I must dress appropriately to receive such a guest. I will meet him in the reception hall as soon as possible. Inform the kitchen that we will have a guest for dinner in the house and others in the guard barracks. Ask Helen to assign someone to see to Fair's needs.

"Then run up to the Matron and inform her. Say that I hope for her presence at dinner this evening."

"Yes, Honor. It will be as you say." Daniel bowed and hurried away.

I turned and spoke to Heather. "Sister! Your fondest wishes are granted! Lars has decided to pay us an unannounced visit."

She looked startled, and then grinned happily. "And I'm getting clean just in time! I can't wait to—" she stopped, looked exaggeratedly concerned. "But will I even be allowed to spend time alone with him? Will you steal him from me to talk business all night?"

"I think you'll have your time alone. I would have to tie him to a chair to keep him from your waiting arms. However, I will insist that you join us for dinner tonight, so dress appropriately."

I turned to Tsha as I donned my bath robe. "You also will dress for dinner. Look your best, my pretty lover. Fair has a fine eye for beauty, and I don't want him disappointed. However, before that please run up to Mother and offer your assistance if needed for bathing, dressing, or anything else." I gave her a quick kiss and hurried to my rooms.

We greeted each other with the warrior's handshake and a clap on the shoulder. It was good to see him again. Lars was shorter than me, by a little, but had skills that I could not match. His blonde hair marked him as coming from northern stock. His great grandparents had settled Fair Keep and they had thrived. We had been friends since childhood. He had assumed his title two years earlier after a Kursh assassin killed his father. Lars had tracked the assassin into Kursh territory and caught him less than a mile from a Kursh garrison. He had gagged his enemy, tied him up, and brought him back to the Keep. The man had ridden the seventy miles draped over the back of a horse.

Fair had declined to give me the details of the execution. His mother and grandmother had arranged it, and apparently it abolished any notion about the female being the gentler sex.

I bowed first, as was custom, since he was my guest. "Fair, my House is blessed by your presence. It has been too long since your last visit."

He returned the bow. "Honor, I am blessed by your welcome. It is indeed too long since I have availed myself of your hospitality."

Then he straightened up and grinned. "Well! Now that we have that nonsense out of the way, let's get a drink. That is, if you think you can drag yourself away from the courtship of your little slave girl."

"'Courtship,' eh? I take it you've communicated with Heather recently?"

"I decline to name my sources. I may need them later. The other three are having a good laugh about it as well. Why bother, Brother? You can have her when you want her, and as often. Or have you gone even softer as you age?" He was grinning as he said this.

"No, it's not that. Lars, I am looking at this in the long term."

He sobered at once. "Long term? You are saying that this is the one, then?"

"She is Aelfir, so, yes, she is the one. My instincts told me that it would be best if I allowed her time. The 'courtship' is over, and was quite successful."

He shook his head. "Collin, just because you will marry her does not mean you needed to fall in love with her."

Before I could protest he held up his hand. "Don't even try to deny it. It is written in your eyes and your voice as clearly as the words on the paper that hold that damn prophecy." He shook his head. "You bear a large burden, Brother. But I can think of no one more able to carry it."

"Haven't you said that before?"

"I believe before I said only better you than me. Come, Collin, let's have that drink. This visit is more business than social. We have matters to discuss."

I continued the conversation as we strolled to the side board area of the dining room.

"You dream, Lars. The two female members of my family know of your arrival. They will join us for dinner and I can assure you that the evening will be social. We have an hour to discuss business before then, and anything left will have to wait till the morning. Heather already expressed concern that she would not have time alone with you because of business."

"Heh! Well, since you put it that way, I suppose much of our business can wait until tomorrow. I certainly would not want your beautiful charming sister to be disappointed."

I poured us both a strong drink. As I handed him the cup, I asked, "That being the case, do you wish to wash off the dust of the road before dinner?"

He thought for a second. "Perhaps I should. Perhaps Heather would like to help me with that, even."

"Not likely. She just got out of the bath, and I suspect Mother is just now getting in. We had opportunity to get a little messy a few hours ago."

"So I have heard. On our way we saw in the distance two Kursh wagons heading due east, along with extra horses and a small company of your men. Of course we had to investigate. Another assassination attempt?"

"And/or an attempt to get Tsha—my Aelfir slave girl—or kill her. Turg still tries to foil prophecy."

"So Heather has been blooded. Excellent. I will make it a point to congratulate her ... privately, at least."

"Lars, what you and my sister do in the privacy of her quarters, or yours, is strictly between the two of you. However, I must point out that if you were to break her heart I would be bound by obligation and tradition to extract satisfaction. And it would be messy."

"And what if, Brother, she breaks my heart? What would you do then?"

"In the unlikely event that your heart is vulnerable to that kind of breakage, I would most certainly give her a harsh scolding."

"So she gets a scolding, but I get a blade in the belly? Hardly seems just."

"Lars, you are my closest and oldest friend. I would put a blade in my own belly before I put one in yours. No, I was thinking of a more minor wound a little farther down. And with luck, the pain and disability would only be temporary."

We both shared a good laugh then and sipped quietly for a while. Then an important matter occurred to me.

"We were speaking of the prophecy. Lars, Tsha knows nothing even of its existence. I wish to keep it that way, so mind your speech."

"Why so? I would think she has the right to know."

I explained my reasons and, after brief contemplation, he agreed. "You have an excellent point, Collin. We allow the damn thing to control us even more than it might. There should be at least one key figure in its tale that acts without its influence.

"Collin, while we still have a few minutes, I'll bring up my reason for the visit. We missed you two weeks ago at the gathering. Usually you are the one that sends out messengers to remind us. This time, no messengers and then, no Honor. And no word as to why. I will admit we were all concerned for your welfare, despite the prophecy.

"Then I discovered that you were courting a slave girl picked up in that skirmish with the dung eaters. But we still heard nothing from you, so I decided if Honor would not come to the Brotherhood, one of the Brotherhood must come to Honor.

"My purpose is to bring you back—drag you if necessary—to Center. The others will be there—again—and we will make up for the time missed.

"Besides, Collin, your men missed you. They see you so seldom as it is, and then you disappointed them. We were able to allay their fears, but not their dissatisfaction. Only you can do that.

"Oh, and more thing even more immediately important." He held out his empty cup. "How about a refill?"

"Depends. If you wish to bathe before dinner, or even just throw some water on your face and arms, you'd best do that first. Also, this stuff is rather potent. You'll do better to enjoy the second with food. If you demonstrate even a hint of drunkenness, it will be a long time before Heather forgives either of us."

"Good point." He set the cup on the board. "Have I time for an actual bath before dinner?"

"I'll instruct Helen to hold service a few extra minutes. Don't dawdle. I can assure you that the three beautiful ladies that will share the meal with us are quite hungry, as am I. Take too long and we'll start without you, and you can catch up at the servants' table in the kitchen."

"Motivation indeed!" With that grinning exclamation he turned and actually trotted from the room.

I followed my own advice and did not help myself to more drink. Instead I went to the kitchen and expressed my wishes to Helen. She would relay the plans upstairs to the ladies. The servant she had assigned to assist our guest would keep her informed as to when the meal should be prepared and ready.

I sat in the dining room for a while, chatting with Daniel about the day's events. The next person to join me in the dining room was, to my slight surprise, Captain Halyar, wearing his finest dress uniform. Without direction from me, Daniel exited and presumably took his place just inside the kitchen where he would have his meal.

Halyar bowed and looked faintly uncomfortable.

"I take it Mother invited you to dinner?"

"Yes, Sir, if that's all right."

"More than all right, Captain! It has been too long since you did us the honor of dining with us. Besides, I wouldn't dare dispute any guest of the Matron. I may be the supposed head of this house, but I'm not crazy.

"Two quick bits of business, Captain, before the others arrive. I'm going to be leaving with Fair in the morning for Center. When you are done here, please select six to accompany us."

"Of course, Honor. Anyone specific?"

"Grolin, of course, for the competition. Beyond that I trust your judgment. The other thing is, absolutely no talk of a prophecy tonight. The subject is off limits. We wish to keep the conversation light and cheerful."

"Suits me," Fair said as he entered the room. "I am pleased you haven't started without me. I was afraid I'd be eating in the kitchen."

Mother's voice alerted us of her presence. "Oh, Fair, we would never allow such an honored guest to be so displaced. Better that we all go hungry."

We three men turned to the opposite entrance of the dining room. The three ladies had entered together. They bowed as one, smiling victoriously at the stunned expressions our faces suddenly bore. All three were beautiful.

Halyar stared, and then looked uncertainly to me. "Honor, are these the same warriors that took Kursh lives earlier today, and allowed themselves to be splashed by the blood of their enemies?"

"Yes, I believe they are. They clean up well, don't they?"

Mother didn't miss a beat. "As do you gentlemen. You especially, Collin. You were sporting more red than anyone else."

I bowed in acknowledgement.

Heather had to speak up. "He certainly was! In fact, they both were. The bath water was pink when they finished. They had to use another tub to rinse!"

I stepped forward and made formal introduction. "Fair, this is Tsha, my companion. Tsha, this is the leader of Fair Keep, my very good friend, and the keeper of my sister's heart ... at least, for the moment."

Tsha bowed formally. "Fair, it is a true privilege to meet one that Honor holds in such high regard."

Fair returned the bow (probably the only time in his life he bowed to a slave), "It is my true pleasure to meet such a beautiful lady. It is clear why Honor has chosen you to be his companion."

Helen hurried into the room, spoke quietly with Mother, received a nod, and hurried out.

"Gentlemen," Mother suggested happily, "if you will seat your ladies, dinner will be served."

7

CHE MAGIC

"COLLIN, MY FOREVER LOVE, I understand there is a special day coming soon." We had made love. I lay on my back. Her head pillowed on my chest, we shared intimacy and gentle touches.

"Really? What day is that?"

"The day that marks your eighth year as Honor. A day of celebration for the Keep, the town, and your friends that govern the rest of the Free Peoples. Is that not correct?"

I sighed. "Yes, that is correct, although we do not consider it so celebratory a day as do others. For our family, it is more a day of remembrance for my father's passing."

"But it is also a day of gifting, is it not?"

"That has been the tradition for generations. Why?"

She turned her head and looked into my eyes. "I feel that I should give you something. Yet, I am only a slave. I own nothing, save the clothes I wear when I dine with you, and the bracelet the Matron allowed me to have this afternoon. And those are all gifts."

"Tsha, the bracelet was not a gift. You earned that with your service and your duel. More important, you have already given me your heart, your beautiful self, your trust, your love. What could you possibly give me that would be more wonderful than that?"

She smiled brightly. "I could give you a son."

She moved herself on top of me, lying with her whole length upon mine, her lips seductively close. "It would bring me great joy to gift you with our son."

I had not expected that. I felt almost faint, and my throat swelled suddenly with a joyous love that threatened to overwhelm me. I did not allow myself to surrender to that, but it was difficult. I did have to wait a few minutes before answering, so that I would not betray myself.

"Tsha, I am sorry, but I could not acknowledge a child born to a slave as my heir. It simply would not be allowed. The child would be free, but could not be an heir."

"Oh." She was crestfallen. She laid the side of her face on my chest and allowed me to feel her disappointment.

"However, if my son was born to a free woman that had once been a slave, and had consented to marry me after becoming free, then the boy would certainly be my official son and heir. And that would indeed be a great gift."

She stopped breathing. She tensed herself into immobility and held herself still for a very long moment.

"Master, do you suggest that your slave might be freed so that you can have an official heir?"

"No. I suggest that my slave might be freed because I love her more than I love myself. I would have you free, Tsha, so that our marriage could be official. I would be proud, Tsha, happy and very proud to have you stand beside me as my wife."

She looked up at me then, with a love I could not resist.

"Tsha, as of this moment you are no longer slave. You are a free woman, a citizen of Honor Keep, and a welcome member of my family. It cannot be official until announced publicly, but for us, you, me, Mother and Heather, it will be fact."

Her beautiful lavender eyes filled with tears, but her expression spoke only of joy. She said nothing.

"Now that you are free, and free to make decisions about yourself and your future, I must ask. Tsha, will you consent to be my wife?"

No response. Just joy mixed with puzzlement and undying love reflected in her tear-filled eyes. Finally, hesitantly, she answered. "Collin, I have been a slave for a long time. Not once in over five years have I been permitted to make a decision about anything. Not even by you. Though you have treated me as an equal in most things, still it has been clear that I was your slave and subject to your decisions. Even my treatment of you as an equal and as a free lover was because you wished it so.

"And now you ask me to make a decision of this importance. Perhaps you will allow me to make a few small decisions first, about small things, before I have to make such a large one?"

It was my turn to hesitate. I admit that I had expected immediate and enthusiastic consent. I was disappointed.

But she was right. To force upon her the biggest decision of her life (it was even bigger than she could imagine—damned prophecy) as the first decision she'd made in over five years was not only unfair, but impractical. Besides, even women free their whole lives often hesitate over the marriage decision.

"You are right, Tsha. Answer me when you are sure, though I hope that will be before the day of remembrance. In the meantime, a much smaller decision is required. Would you consent to make love to me again? Right now?"

That decision, at least, was an easy one.

Some hours later after we had loved and slept, she said softly, "Collin, may I ask a question?"

"You know that you do not need permission."

"You are the leader of the Free Peoples, and the Free Lands. Why do you call yourselves such and yet keep slaves? It seems to me a contradiction."

That was certainly a question I had not anticipated. Those things I took for granted since they had been so my whole life. I had to actually think about it for a minute or so.

I stroked her hair absently as I spoke slowly, choosing my words before I released them.

"We are the Free Lands and the Free Peoples because we have no king, no lord, no single ruler to which we owe allegiance. Each Keep is a separate free entity. We are answerable to each other only to the extent of security of the entire Free Lands. For example, as I have said, no slave is forced to have sex with anyone in Honor Keep, and even attempted rape is not tolerated. My grandfather first put forth the idea, my father implemented it and I have continued that philosophy. Trust Keep has a somewhat looser view of what constitutes forced sex and Justice gives fair warning before the enslavement that a slave is expected to grant sexual access when commanded.

"I do not personally approve, but it is none of my business and I would never consider even offering criticism of that condition.

"In addition to that, the cities and towns scattered here and there are free to conduct themselves as they wish, provided they offer no threat to any citizens not within their own territory.

"There was a city in the hills in the north some years ago that became a thieves' stronghold. Robbers, pickpockets, and even murderers took over the town and used it as a refuge from justice. Honest citizenry could not ride the roads without fear of robbery or worse.

"The Brotherhood was reluctant to act because of the history of autonomy allowed. But then one crime was called to their attention and they felt it necessary to take action. The town was burned to the ground and the criminals therein were killed unless they surrendered. Those that surrendered were placed into the harshest possible slavery.

"Which brings us to the second of your concerns. Tsha, most of those that are slaves in the Keeps are so voluntarily. Through dishonesty, or, more often, honest miscalculation or simple bad luck, people acquire debts they have no hope of paying. The Keeps choose not to let the creditors simply suffer the loss when it is not their fault. The Keeps pay the debts but in return the debtors assign themselves as slaves to the Keep for a set period of time. Very few have ever chosen the alternative, which is banishment from the Free Lands. They are given room and board and then beyond that their efforts go to pay back what they owe to the Keep. Usually that span of time is several years.

"One of the hardest things for some of them is the surrender of status. Many were respected citizens, often having been wealthy for a time before misfortune overtook them. As a slave, they have no status. They are no more significant than cattle in the social order."

"That sounds unnecessarily harsh, as if it were a punishment."

"So I thought when it was explained to me when I was a child. But it cannot be any other way. If a person of some importance became a slave but maintained high status it would be much harder for them. They would see themselves as superior to the other slaves and sooner or later they would demonstrate that feeling.

"It would be only days or even hours before the other slaves applied a hard lesson to the offender. So from the very first all slaves realize they have the same status—zero. This serves to protect them from themselves."

"There is still some rank among slaves, but that ranking is established by the owner or the overseer, not by the slaves."

"We have some that choose to stay slaves for the rest of their lives. They find that steady useful work in exchange for room and board is sufficient for them. Almost always these are people who were poor from the beginning and had low status. As a slave, they are equal to all they work with and live with. Some find that quite satisfactory.

"Criminals are also put into slavery as punishment for their crimes. Most are, of course, thieves in some form. The slavery is more severe for those. They are often slept in tents and fed twice a day on meager rations. Their treatment is not at all merciful. Those are sentenced by court to a specific number of years of slavery. After their sentence is served they are released if they have performed well and shown that they are less inclined to return to criminal ways. If they do not demonstrate such a change they are escorted beyond the borders of the Free Lands and told that their return will result in their execution.

"Presently, Honor Keep has no criminal slaves. At the same time, Truth Keep has nearly a dozen. Some thought that when Truth inherited his position at such a young age they had an opportunity to get away with bad behavior. They soon learned better.

"And, lastly, there are those that were slaves when they came into the care of the Keep. Most are like you, Tsha, slaves of the Kursh and acquired as spoils of battle.

"I know that you wonder why we simply don't free them. There are reasons. First, we feel some responsibility to them. Slavery in Honor Keep, as you now know, is not harsh. It is felt that granting them a place to live safely and feeding them in return for their labor is a fair exchange until they demonstrate that they will be able to be productive citizens when freed. Some, like you, simply have nowhere else to go.

"Also, we have no idea initially what kind of people such slaves might be. Like us, the Kursh enslave criminals, though more often they just kill them. But we do not wish to simply allow criminals to wander loosely within the Free Lands. Their slavery with us is like a probationary period.

"You will have been formally freed in less than five months from your first acquisition by Honor Keep. That is almost unheard of. Most will wait eight months at the very least. But you have earned your freedom even if I had not fallen in love with you. The increased production in the fields and orchards and the beautification of the garden has been easily enough to warrant your freedom. In addition, you have shown yourself trustworthy and honest. Clearly you will be an outstanding and productive citizen of the Free Lands."

I kissed her softly on the forehead. "And, if you consent, you will make an outstanding Lady of Honor Keep."

She said nothing, but sighed and snuggled herself even closer against me and we slept.

She woke me again later as she changed position and kissed me softly on the chin in passing.

I asked her, "Tsha, do you recall our conversation in the orchard?"

She thought for a few seconds. "Yes. You were wondering if I could use my lips, or feet, or anything other than my hands for what you call the death touch."

"The Aelfir do not call it that?"

"No. Collin, it is our defense, and that is what it is called. Simply our defense and nothing more."

"Hmm! I have learned something new. Tsha, in the morning I will leave with Lars for Center. I will be gone four days, perhaps more. I ask you to do a few things while I am gone. First, continue to train with the spear, and work even harder at that task. Second, and most important, I need you to try very hard to administer your defense through your lips. A death kiss, if you will. The future holds many possibilities, and the Kursh may decide to wage war upon us at any time though we do keep a close eye on them. But it is my duty to prepare for all eventualities I can conceive. I need to know if you can do such a thing. And third, I want you also to extend your magic, to tax it to its farthest limits."

"In what way, my love?"

"I would be very interested to see if you can cause growth in plant fibers that are long dead. See if you can cause hemp rope, for example, or the bamboo in the fences, to grow, or even to stretch. Will you do these things for me?"

"Of course I will, though I cannot promise success, except that I will improve my skills with the spear. The others are things foreign to the nature of my people. But you have already forced me to violate that nature, and I feel no worse in my heart for it. I think your love has helped me with that. So, yes, Collin, Honor, former master, companion, lover, I will do my very best for you. But I ask one thing in return."

She looked very earnestly into my eyes and put her hand to my face. "Be careful and alert, and come back to me unharmed. I know that you will be traveling where it should be safe. But I will worry for you none the less."

I chuckled and hugged her tight, and kissed her very well. "Tsha, you can be sure that I will use all caution. I owe you the official ceremony declaring your freedom, and I would not deny you that."

She kissed me back then with a passion somehow different than before … perhaps the passion of a free woman rather than that of a slave.

8

THE BROTHERHOOD

W E LEFT A SHORT TIME BEFORE SUNRISE. We cantered the horses for the ten miles of Honor land, and then allowed them to walk for several miles before picking up the pace again. At that rate we would reach Center about sunset.

Lars and I mostly engaged in small talk during the times we walked the horses, much of it having to do with the excellence of our lady loves. Lars was discreet enough not to give me details about the "excellence" of my little sister, and I declined to reveal the detail of Tsha's magical touch, but we did both speak of what our hearts felt for those young ladies. It pleased me to know that my friend was as devotedly smitten with Heather as Heather was with him.

But there was one little bit of conversation that was not small talk.

"Collin, there is one detail you should be aware of before we join the others. Lucas has a problem. Or perhaps it would be more accurate to say that we have a problem with Lucas. He has become addicted to drink. He is always with a bottle in his hand now, and he is a drunk."

"That's why you came yourself to fetch me to Center so urgently."

"That is why I wanted you in Center so urgently, yes. I came personally for other reasons."

I had never had much experience dealing with drunks. My father, however, had dealt with many over the years, and had written extensively about his experience. There are three kinds. There is the happy drunk, the hostile drunk, and the stupefied drunk.

"Which kind of drunk is he?"

"Loud, surly, and impolite."

"Yes, that does sound like a problem."

We rode in silence for a good while, urging the horses back to the faster pace. We stopped at a river for rest, water, and food. I had used the time of silence to contemplate the problem. I waited until we had seated ourselves upon the ground to take our meal.

"Lars, when we arrive I need you to tell the other two Brothers, on the sly of course, that they must not interfere in any way with the confrontation. No matter what happens Lucas must never feel that we are all against him. It must be strictly between him and me."

"You anticipate trouble with him?"

"Of course! Taking his bottle from a drunk always causes trouble, or so Father has written. It must be done with reckless care. Can you restrain yourself, and make sure they do likewise? Trust me as you have in the past?"

He looked at me curiously. "Of course, Collin. How else? Do we not always follow your lead?"

"In battle, yes, for all of you appointed me your commander. But this is not battle. This is the Brotherhood. We are equals in assemblage."

"Collin, one thing we all love about you is that you actually believe what you just said. But the rest of us know that you are our leader, our commander, not just on the field, but anytime and anywhere. We follow your lead because, as your father before you, you have shown a brilliance for strategy that none of us can match, and we all know it.

"I'll admit that it seems unjust to me that one man has not only the best of brains among us, but also the most skill with bow and sword." He grinned. "But I try hard not to resent you for it." He looked at the sky. "Come, we best get going to arrive before sunset. We don't want Steven at Center worrying about us."

It was indeed nearing sunset when we arrived at Center Keep. Center is under the control of the Brotherhood jointly, for use at the discretion of each for personal matters. Its primary purpose is a staging and training area for the joint forces of the Free Peoples. Each of the five Keeps contributes about a thousand men to the amassed army and sends wagonloads of food and other supplies on a regular basis or as needed, plus payment to the soldiers, of course.

Besides the cities associated closely with each of the Keeps, there are many smaller towns and one large city scattered throughout the Free Lands. All contributed to the army of the Free Peoples, both with goods and with personnel. The total number of trained soldiers the Free Peoples could call upon for war was several thousand. Still, that was fewer than what the Kursh would be able to amass. This was one of those factors I always had to consider when planning what was to come. I did not worry about it, though; there was little I could do to enhance our numbers and that little was already in process.

As with the other Keeps, a city was close to Center Keep, and much of its economy was dependent on the garrison. Besides the usual weavers and tailors and grocers and butchers there were more than the usual number of smiths and doctors and shops for weapons and tack, plus hostels for visitors. And what army town would be complete without a brothel or three?

And many of the adult men and women of the town were also reservists, to be called up for the service in support capacities at least if needed. And some might find themselves thrown into the front lines at some point.

Our company split up when we arrived. Our guards went first to the stables, taking our two horses after we removed our personal items. They would then take themselves to the barracks and be on their own time until called upon. They would certainly spend plenty of time and money in the city.

Lars and I entered the Keep without fanfare, but were greeted enthusiastically by Richard and Steven. Lucas's greeting was more restrained.

I greeted them formally, Richard first. "Trust! It has been too long! My spirit is renewed by your company and the Brotherhood is strengthened by our mutual presence."

Richard was the oldest of the Brotherhood. He was, in fact, old enough to be the father of Lars, Steven, or me. He was larger than all of us as well, and even darker of complexion than the Kursh. His ancestors had come from the far south, beyond the desert. When they settled in the southwestern part of the Free Lands it was not long before they came in contact with Steven's ancestors and then those of mine and Lucas. Lars's ancestors had not yet come into the country. Those men and women had all found they had certain things in common. They had similar values; values that were in direct opposition to the culture of the Kursh.

It was that situation which caused the Keeps to be named as they were: to remind the descendants of their values, and to emphasize the difference between the values of the Free Peoples and those of the Kursh.

Richard had been titled since before I was born. His father had actually died purely by accident, which was the exception among us. The rest of us lost our fathers to the Kursh, one way or another.

"Honor! The Brotherhood is again strengthened by your presence. You have been sorely missed, and I delight in your company."

We exchanged bows, then the handclasps of warriors, and a companionable clap on the shoulder.

Truth and I greeted each other with the same words and actions. Steven was our youngest. He was barely nineteen and the unhappiest of us all. When a Kursh assassin killed his father Steven was only eleven and no one from Truth Keep had been able to catch the killer. Steven hated the Kursh with a vehemence that outmatched even Tsha's hatred; he felt that every Kursh might be his father's killer. In the battles against them since he became old enough to be on the field, he could not kill enough of them to satisfy himself, and the rest of the Brotherhood had found it necessary to convince him that he was not free to go berserk upon the enemy without regard to his own welfare.

Justice stepped forward. He put the bottle in his hand upon the table so he could greet me properly. We bowed and greeted each other with the same words and gestures as the other two but his speech held a bare hint of slurring. I noticed that Lars had spoken quietly and hurriedly to the other two.

As soon as the greetings were finished Lucas retrieved his bottle and pulled a long drink from it.

Lucas looked terrible. He had lost weight, and it was clearly muscle that had disappeared, since he'd had little fat. He had kept himself as sharply well-conditioned as the rest of us. There were dark circles under his eyes and his black hair was longer than he usually wore it. He had not shaved in days, but I did not think he was intentionally growing a beard. I was the only one of us that kept that unfashionable fashion, and I had good reason.

The kitchen steward entered and asked if dinner could be served. We all exchanged glances, no one declined, so we adjourned to the dining area and took our seats. The table was rectangular and had room for six, though only five had ever occupied it at one time since I had first taken my place there.

I steered Lucas to the end chair and sat myself on his left on the long side. The other three took their places as they saw fit. Steven sat on my left with Richard across from him and Lars on Lucas's right. This did help assure that Steven and Richard would not interfere.

We engaged in conversation during the meal. My Brothers insisted on hearing as many details as I was willing to share about the beautiful slave I'd been "courting," and I revealed to them all that she was certainly the one prophesied.

Conversation continued with light-hearted banter and we finished the meal. Lucas did not take part. He ate little and drank from his bottle much too much. I waited until we had all finished and the dishes were cleared from the table.

I could tell that the others were waiting for me. I think perhaps even Lucas was waiting. I could not disappoint them.

The next time Lucas raised the bottle to his lips I reached across him with my left hand and intercepted the motion and did not permit it to reach his lips.

He was surprised, then immediately angry. He strained to overpower my left hand with his right, but he could not. The bottle waved up and down and forward and back in the air, sloshing a little from the mouth, but came no closer to his lips. He turned red and became furious.

"Get your damned hand off, Collin, or you will lose it!"

I looked him squarely in the eyes and answered calmly. "No. It is time for your hand to release the poison, Lucas."

He struggled again but could not break my grip nor overcome my arm. "Damn you! I will kill you if you do not let go!"

His left hand flashed to his right side and he pulled his knife from his belt and held the blade to my throat, much as I had done to the Kursh only the day before.

I did not waver, but held his eyes.

"Lucas, this is no good. Every time you drink from the bottle, the bottle drinks from you. It has taken over your will, and your mind. You have become nothing more than a slave to the liquor."

He struggled again to defeat my grasp. I had carefully kept my own right hand upon the table, gripping the edge to help support me in the struggle. I felt him push the knife blade against my skin.

"Look at yourself, Lucas. You hold a knife to the throat of your sworn Brother. The liquor has become more sacred to you than your very oath! Has the drug turned your love to hate so easily? Would you treat me as no more than a hated Kursh?"

I could feel then his left hand begin to tremble. He looked away from my eyes and to the knife, actually realizing for the first time what he was doing. He snatched his hand away from my throat and allowed the knife to drop onto the table.

I spoke urgently.

"Lucas, I need you! The Brotherhood needs you. We need you whole, and sober, and at your best. The end is not soon, but it is in sight.

"Lucas, we will not win without you at your best. You must put aside the drink. Now."

I took my hand from the bottle and allowed him to do what he would with it.

Lars began, "Collin —"

I gestured at Lars to hold his piece. He reached a lap cloth across the table to me. I glanced at him and he gestured to his own throat. I put the cloth to my throat where the blade had been. It came away bloody, but not too badly. Just a nick.

Lucas had slumped in his chair and was staring at nothing, the bottle held slackly in his hand, resting in his lap. He saw the exchange and looked at me and saw the blood on my throat. His eyes grew wide. He looked at the knife blade and saw there was blood upon it. He was horrified.

He jumped to his feet, shouted a wordless expression of grief and shame, and hurled the bottle at the empty fireplace across the room. It shattered.

The rest of us were able to relax. Just to be cautious, though, I moved the knife out of his reach. I gave him a few minutes to come to grips with himself while I pressed the cloth against the nick. The bleeding stopped.

"Lucas, Brother, where is the rest?"

He looked startled, then ashamed. "My quarters."

"Let's go get it all."

He was not enthusiastic, but agreed, and motioned us to follow. In his room concealed by a cloth throw was a cask with the bung near the bottom. Next to it was another bottle, full. Obviously Lucas's addiction was so compelling that he always had a second bottle ready for drink.

I reached for the bottle, then stopped and asked. "Lucas, may I?"

His eyes darted from my hand to the bottle to the cask to my face and back to the bottle. He licked his lips and suddenly looked desperately thirsty. But he nodded.

I took the bottle and pulled the stopper and took a small cautious drink. It had a pleasant taste, but in mere seconds I could feel the impact on my senses. It was almost staggering! I wanted to sit down, my vision blurred, and my ears rang.

The effect lasted only a minute. But I found, disconcerting as the effect had been, that I wanted another drink! A bigger one this time. I shook my head and firmly replaced the stopper and set it on the table.

"Lucas, I am sure that what I just had is not what you first tasted. Where did you get it?"

He looked sheepish. "Kursh traders. They urged me to try a bottle. It was a gift. It tasted just fine, and it made me feel good. I purchased three casks. This is the last one, still almost full." He looked at me with miserable shame. "I am sorry, Collin. It seemed harmless."

I nodded. "They diluted the first bottle to allow you to get used to it. This is not a drink; it is a drug. They intentionally addicted you to it, to weaken the Brotherhood. They have been unsuccessful at killing us, so they try other tactics."

Lucas seemed bemused as he absently reached for the bottle, uncorked it, and took it to his mouth.

"Lucas!" All four of us spoke sharply at once. He looked startled, and then realized what he was doing. With difficulty he replaced the cork. His face became red.

"I will kill them! I will take them back to Justice and skin them alive. And pour their damned drug onto their exposed flesh! I will cut off their—"

"Lucas—"I interrupted, "before you get too involved with your plans for revenge, what can you tell us about these Kursh traders? Do you remember a name?"

"Of course. The leader's name was Dort. Clean-shaven they were, which was odd, but they were all dressed as traders and had the goods you'd expect. Why? Did you encounter them?"

"Yes. And you can put aside your plans for your just revenge. They are all back in Kursh by now. At least, their bodies are in Kursh. I have no idea in which part of hell their spirits might reside."

He looked both disappointed and somewhat appeased. "Honor Keep killed them?"

"Yes, every one. You can relax. Justice may not have brought about their end, but they paid for their sins none the less."

I stepped to him and put my hand on his shoulder. "I am more worried about you. This is a powerful drug. You are going to have a difficult time weaning yourself from it suddenly. You may need help."

"I will have it. Ruth will help. I have been worthless as husband and father since I took that first drink. I realize that now. But she will help me, and I will devote myself to making it up to her and my son. But what shall we do with that damned poison?"

I'd been thinking about that.

"We'll give it to Lars."

"Oh, we will, eh? And why do I get the loser's prize?"

"Because you, Lars, are the most talented scout in the Free Lands. We know you could slip into Turg's tent, cut a piece of hair from his head, and slip back out without ever being seen."

He laughed. "I am good, Collin, but not quite that good. Besides, why would I want to cut his hair when I could cut his throat?"

The rest of us laughed as well, even Lucas, which was a good sign. "Good point. But what I had in mind was you taking the cask and bottle as close as possible to Turg's current location and dumping it all in his water source. It came from him originally I'm sure, so we should return it."

After a few seconds of silence and exchanged looks, they gifted me with delighted grins and applause.

Richard said, "Wonderful! Collin, that is why you are our commander! You have such excellent ideas!"

I gave a flamboyant bow to him to acknowledge the compliment. Then I very firmly grasped the cask, hoisted it onto my shoulder, and carried it back to my own quarters. Lars followed with the bottle. Lucas followed, and Steven and Richard brought up the rear.

Each of the rooms had a small closet that could be locked. We almost never bothered with locking them, but this time I used it for the cask and bottle. I didn't want Lucas tempted beyond his capacity. He was a strong man, a stubborn man, but the one small swallow I sampled convinced me that the drug was strong, too. The addiction might be even stronger than his will.

After I had locked them up, adding a bit of ceremony to the process, I turned to Lucas and clapped him on the shoulder.

"You're going to find yourself getting thirsty. Take a bucket of water into your room tonight. Sleep will come hard, too." I looked around at the rest of the Brotherhood. I grinned. "If you need to talk to someone tonight, feel free to wake one of us. Except me."

They all laughed shortly, and then three of them dispersed. Steven stayed.

"Collin, may we speak privately?"

"Certainly, Brother. Let's return to the dining area if that is acceptable. I'd like some strong tea to get the last taste of that drug out of my mouth."

"Certainly. A cup of strong tea sounds good in any case."

"That is a potent drug, Steven. Nasty stuff. Too bad that those Kursh are already dead. Our Brother would have punished them much more severely than the honorable deaths they received."

When the kitchen staff had fetched our cups and we were seated, I invited Steven to speak his mind.

"Collin, my question is simple. How do you have the control you showed this evening? Justice held a knife to your throat. He was angry, not in real control of himself, and he even drew blood. Yet, you did not twitch or even blink. I watched you. Your breathing did not even increase! How can you have that kind of courage?"

I took a drink while I pondered the answer.

"Steven, I thank you for the compliment, but it was not courage you witnessed so much as faith—or, if you prefer the word, trust."

"How could you trust Lucas that completely? He was not himself."

"No, I did not mean that I had faith in Lucas. I trusted to the Prophecy! It states quite clearly that I will be alive and able to fight well almost two years from now. So I knew I was in no real danger."

"Collin, as you know, I have never read the Prophecy, nor heard it told. I have merely heard you and Lars, or very seldom the other two make reference to it. And almost always it is called 'that damned Prophecy.' If it is so reassuring, why do you and Lars, especially, curse it so often?"

Again I had to ponder before I answered.

"Steven, over the course of the last one hundred years my family, each generation, has attempted in some way to foil or negate the Prophecy. Each attempt has not only failed, but resulted in tragedy.

"As you know, the prophecy does indicate that I will marry an Aelfir slave and we will have a son. Beyond that, you do not need to know more. Richard knows more. He was Father's good friend, as Lars is mine. But the fewer that know the details, the better. I prefer that foreknowledge not influence decisions. Lucas has never shown much interest in the Prophecy, and I have hoped that you would be likewise.

"Not important. Let me give you an example. When I was your age I fell in love. She was a farm girl I saw in town one afternoon. She was there with her family, doing the weekly shopping. She was eighteen, beautiful, with long fragrant hair the color of ripe corn and eyes like the clearest sky. A smile that held the warmest sunshine you've ever felt, and kisses that ... well, never mind. I courted her. We fell in love. Mother warned me, but I thought I knew better. I would marry this girl and the Prophecy be damned! I asked and she accepted.

"Three days later she was killed. Just an accident with a wagon and runaway horses on a muddy road. I've often wondered if I hadn't insisted on marrying her, if she'd still be alive, loving another man, raising children, keeping her part of the world a happier place.

"You can see why I curse the Prophecy. Yes, it is useful sometimes. But it is easily more a curse than a blessing."

He was quiet, solemn, even sad for me, I think.

"Was that all that was on your mind, Steven, or do other things trouble you?"

"Just one, I guess, right now. Honor, does the Prophecy mention me?"

"Not specifically. It has a little general mention of the leaders of the Keeps, but only as a group. Not as individuals. Honor Keep is the only one of the Keeps that the Prophecy mentions with any detail, and that too much." We stood up, tea unfinished. "We should sleep, Brother. We have a busy day tomorrow."

"Yes, we do! I forgot. Sorry, Collin, I should not have kept you up."

"Nonsense! We do not talk nearly often enough. The strength of the Brotherhood is far more important than one good night's sleep."

"I'm glad you think so, Collin," Lucas remarked as he entered. "I can't sleep."

"By a happy coincidence, Justice, Truth is also very much awake. The two of you have more in common than you might suspect, and this is an excellent opportunity to find that you may be brothers in spirit as well as in oath. And, being young, Steven will be able to survive tomorrow on a short night.

"I, however, need to catch several hours of sleep before tomorrow's entertainment." I bowed. "Good even to you both," and I hurried to my rooms. As I learned the next day, the two talked well into the night. Steven learned a few things from his older Brother, and Lucas got through his first sober night in months.

9

ᴄʜᴇ ᴄᴏɴᴄᴇꜱᴄꜱ

I T HAD BEEN TRADITION FOR A LONG TIME to have games of skill at the gatherings of the Brotherhood—not just for the commanders of the Keeps, but for their soldiers as well. My absence two weeks earlier had disrupted the planned games. Without my presence, the warriors from Honor Keep were not free to compete. The Brotherhood had postponed the games, and now that I was present all the competitors were eager to get started.

We of the Brotherhood were free to compete or not, as we preferred. But there was peer pressure to demonstrate our expertise with weaponry. Among other things, it was necessary to reassure our soldiers that we could at least hold our own on the field.

With age, Richard had grudgingly admitted that he no longer had the quickness to successfully compete with sword or spear, or even with the bow competition. But he still participated successfully in the distance-with-accuracy bow game; so successfully that he remained the champion after this year's games.

Lucas simply declined, with a frank apology to his company. They had heard the rumors of his affliction. He admitted it, declared the affliction over, but admitted he was not physically fit to participate this time. He was the current champion of the javelin, where distance and accuracy—the weapon was thrown into a man-shaped target—determined the winner. The javelin was no longer a much-used weapon. The Kursh would retrieve the weapon and use it against us. But we still held the competition as a nod to tradition though each year fewer warriors entered that particular contest. Richard had been runner-up the previous year. It was expected that he would win the competition in Lucas's absence, but he was surprisingly defeated by three smaller men—all archers. This stirred the beginning of an idea in the back of my thoughts, but it did not then force itself into my concerns.

Steven, Lars, and I participated fully. Steven had not yet achieved a championship in any of the contests, but he was still young and lacked both the physical maturity and the practice time necessary to become elite. But he enjoyed competing, took his losses in good spirits, and maintained the respect of his soldiers. And he improved his standing with each subsequent competition.

Lars was reigning runner-up with the spear, but he was a long-standing champion in weaponless combat. He combined strength with a flexible agility that no one else could quite match.

He was unable to improve his standing with the spear. He was out-dueled by a woman from his own Keep. He retained his status in the weaponless combat trials.

I was fortunate enough to be the current champion in two events: speed archery and the sword. In the first event, the object was to hit the man-shaped target with as many fatal arrows as possible within a specified period of time from fifty paces.

In the previous contest, I had actually come in second in the number of arrows delivered, but all of mine had hit vital areas. My opponent—a sergeant from Truth Keep—had delivered three more arrows, but one missed entirely and two had been judged as not qualifying as kill shots. He did better this year while my effort was the same. We were declared co-winners.

The sword competition always garnered the most interest and the fiercest level of effort. We used sabers dulled at point and edge and then coated with a red chalk bound by tree sap. It left a clear mark on the white shirt of the competitor. The winner was decided by the first "fatal" strike. Then he would be required to change to a clean shirt for the next match, so there would be no confusion about a strike from the previous encounter.

My chief competition was Corporal Grolin from my own Keep's garrison. He'd been the runner-up in the previous three contests, and continued to practice almost maniacally in his determination to unseat me as the champion.

He greeted me specifically before the beginning of the contest. He grinned good-naturedly as he bowed.

"Commander, perhaps this year you will need more than one shirt for the contest."

I grinned back and returned the bow halfway. "Perhaps. If we face each other, the shirt you change into after the match will not need to be white."

He laughed. He was a good sport as well as an excellent swordsman. Captain Halyar had assigned him to be among those whose primary duty was to protect me on the battle field. It was a cherished and honored duty. In our battle with the Kursh that had resulted in the acquisition of several slaves, he and his fellows had had the opportunity to kill many of the enemy. Two of my guard had died protecting me.

We had taken our dead back to the Keep for honorable cremation. The Kursh dead, about a hundred, we had left for the wild dogs, the vultures, the crows, and ultimately the maggots.

At the end of the contest, Grolin remained disappointed. I still needed only the one shirt. He did fight very well, but became too eager when I presented him with what seemed to be an opening. He had done so well that there were no marks on his shirt. There was, however, one on the flesh of his neck with a length and hue indicating a "fatal" blow.

We bowed to each other with equal depth and smiles of congratulations.

There was one weapon that did not rate a contest. That was the short bow. Whereas the long bow was from five to six feet in length, depending on the height of the user, the short bow was about three feet in length. It did not have the range or power of the longbow, of course, but it could be fired much more quickly. It was designed specifically to be used on horseback. Since the Free Peoples had no cavalry and only the commanders rode horses into combat, only the commanders had any use for one. Also, it was not a traditional weapon. My father, Edwin, the third to hold the title of Honor of Honor Keep had developed it specifically for himself and the Brotherhood. And for me. He had insisted that I become as proficient with it as I was with the longbow. I managed to become so and I was quite effective with the weapon while on horseback by the time I was fifteen.

I first used it in battle two years later.

10

CHE DEFEAT

THE KURSH HAVE ON OCCASION been victorious, at least in part. When I was seventeen a small party of Kursh warriors staged a raid on our cattle herd. They split off about two dozen, driving them east toward Kursh. By itself a theft of that size would not have been cause for immediate pursuit and retaliation. Father would have simply sent scouts to follow and observe for days or even weeks if necessary, and when the thieves had settled somewhere we would quietly surround their party and take them hostage, to be executed or sent back to Kursh in exchange for the cattle. That was the normal procedure for such a theft.

But this time they had killed the herders—all six of them, the two herd dogs, and a twelve-year-old boy, the son to one of the herders. When their shift replacements had discovered this, the fastest of them had run the six miles back to the Keep and reported it. Halyar accompanied him to see my father. I remember the tears he shed, and the furious grief he revealed as he told Edwin of the atrocity.

I had seldom seen my father that angry. He sent a servant to fetch his saber from his room and commanded Halyar to have twenty warriors fully armed on horseback in but a few minutes. I ran to my room and grabbed my own saber, and the short bow, and ran out, hoping to join the company.

Elizabeth came out, carrying the saber while the servant hurried along behind. They exchanged quiet words, and I saw Mother wipe tears from her eyes. One of her closest personal servants was wife and mother to two that had been killed.

I saw first Edwin and then Mother look to me. There was no disagreement between them. "Collin," my father commanded, "You will stay close to me. Saddle Gruffy and be quick. We have no time to spare."

"Yes, Sir!" I agreed and ran to the stable—only to find Gruffy already saddled and eager to be off. He was old for a war horse, almost twenty, but was as steady and responsive as any animal we had and experienced in battle. He proudly wore more than one scar from Kursh weapons. We knew each other very well. I had learned to ride on his back, and had already claimed his six-month-old colt, Roughneck, as my own.

Less than an hour after the crime had been discovered Edwin lead the company in grim pursuit of the murderous and thieving Kursh. The tracks of the cattle and the Kursh were easy to follow. It seemed there were perhaps a dozen of them.

Then we saw them as we rounded a hill on our left. Father shouted for us to surge forward and he led the charge.

It was an ambush.

Another dozen Kursh appeared from around the hill, swords drawn or spears ready, and they were in our midst in seconds, fighting us horse to horse and man to man. Their advantage of surprise cost us the lives of four good soldiers in the first two minutes.

Those we had been pursuing turned and charged back against us.

Our warriors reacted perfectly, as Father and Halyar had trained them to do. Father was quickly escorted back next to me and the two of us were surrounded by our warriors. They had their weapons at the ready in seconds, protecting us and killing the Kursh as they came within reach of their swords. Father had an arrow nocked to his short bow in seconds. I froze for perhaps a half minute, then emulated him.

He arrowed one that was getting the best of one of our men and again I copied him. My first kill. I had no time to consider it.

Arrows were suddenly in the air. There were two Kursh archers on the hill and their targets were clearly Honor of Honor Keep and his teenage son. Father noticed them at the same time, and we turned our bows in their direction, but they were hiding behind rocks on the top of the hill. They would pop out, take their shot, and then disappear again while they nocked another arrow.

It was a frozen moment in time. I was looking at the top of the hill, waiting for one of them to present a target. And one did, popping up and loosing an arrow directed straight at me. I loosed my arrow at the same instant.

His arrow may have been aimed perfectly, but I never knew for sure. At the exact same second that I fired, Father's horse shied backward and Father was suddenly between the archer and me. The arrow went through his neck and pierced one of the main blood vessels there. His blood sprayed everywhere. I had time for a flash of vision that showed my arrow pierce the chest of the Kursh archer, then I screamed as I saw my father clutch at his throat and topple from his horse.

I was off Gruffy at once and at Father's side. I paid no attention to the battle around us. But I had only a brief moment to look into my father's eyes and see the light disappear from them. He sighed once and did not breathe again. For the first and last time in my life I did not know what to do. My sudden grief consumed me. I could not believe my father had just died, right there, from an arrow meant for me. An arrow sent by the Kursh.

And then, a minute later, I knew exactly what to do. Grief was replaced by rage. The tears in my eyes and the choking in my throat did not deter me. I drew my sword and took my belt knife in my left hand and waded into the midst of the Kursh, slashing upward at those on horseback, stabbing and cutting and hacking those on foot. I was oblivious to the shouted instructions of our warriors. I resisted their efforts to separate me from the enemy. I had one focus only, and that was to kill Kursh until not a one remained alive.

I was told later, while the healers tended to the few minor wounds on my arms and back, that I had turned the tide of the battle. Only one enemy was taken prisoner—the second archer on the hill. He managed to wound two more warriors; then they charged him faster than he could fire and he was beaten and taken prisoner.

The sergeant, our second in command, asked me what should be done with him. My first thought was to ask Edwin. Then I realized that I could not and the grief and rage surged again within me. Tears streamed from my eyes but there was no shame in it. The sergeant and several others allowed their grief to show as well.

There were no trees on the hill that had hidden the ambush, but east a quarter mile was a smaller hill and that one held a tree perfect for the purpose.

The Kursh was hung from a branch by his neck until he was dead. He faced his homeland. We left him there for the vultures and the flies.

Of the twenty-two that had left Honor Keep only eleven, all wounded, returned alive. Even five of the horses had been killed, but eight of the Kursh horses remained unhurt and we took them back with us, bearing our dead.

After Mother and Heather and I had taken our time to grieve as a family, we joined the rest of the Keep in grieving the loss of all those who had been killed. Edwin received his own funeral pyre while the others shared another. They had all been brothers in arms and had fought and died together. The smoke and ashes from their remains would join together as well, and be mixed so that they remained joined forever.

After that day Mother was the first to address me as Honor. And that was the first time I cursed the Prophecy. It was not nearly the last.

11

THE AELFIR

T HE CONTESTS TOOK THE ENTIRE DAY. After the evening meal we all slept very well ... except Lucas, perhaps. Although I did sleep well, I missed Tsha. I had become used to having her with me in my bed; making love to her before sleep, and sometimes in the night, and even in the morning.

Lars and I could have returned to our respective homes the next morning, but I chose to stay one more day. I needed to get the full picture of our current military standing and projects. Much of it was routine, but there were a few things that held my particular interest.

Immediately after Honor Keep's defeat of the Kursh assassination attempt I had sent a messenger and three of my best scouts to Fair Keep. They joined with three scouts from there and they all skirted the northern border of Kursh to meet with the leadership of the Aelfir, such as they were.

The Aelfir did not have any real organized government and certainly nothing resembling a military force. The Aelfir still lived much as they had for the hundreds of years before the Kursh had arrived from the far south and taken over that land, and at least a hundred years more before the Free Peoples arrived from the southwest, west, and north.

The Aelfir lived in scattered family groupings, most of them isolated from each other. There were a few small villages for trade and meetings, many of those along the eastern coast. The Aelfir that lived there mostly made their living on fish and birds and the various plants and trees that thrived only near the sea. There were also two or three towns of a few hundred in the northern part of Aelf, but generally they were a semi-nomadic race with no history of strife or struggle within their own land. There is little reason to fight when plants and trees can be coaxed into producing as much food as necessary.

This arrangement made it both easier and more difficult for the Kursh to wipe them out. While a family group, once discovered, offered no real resistance to the weapons of the invaders, finding those scattered groups was mostly a matter of chance. And, because the Aelfir were so much a part of their own land, and with the "defense" they had, the outcome was usually as it had been with Tsha and Tchon. The Kursh slew one male, enslaved one female, and lost six of their own in the process.

These constant and increasing invasions of the Kursh had caused the Elders of the Aelfir to consider developing some kind of resistance. But with no weapons and no training in how to use them, there was little they could do.

That is why I sent some of our people to Aelf. Lars and I offered our assistance in training and weapons if they would have it. We would supply bows and arrows and show the Aelfir how to construct their own. The same with spears. There were no metal workers in Aelf, so we did not bother with teaching them use of the sword. A wooden shaft with one end sharpened to a point was nearly as effective as a spear.

Many of the Aelfir, especially the older ones, simply refused to take up the weapons. It was against their nature and they would not—or could not—alter their ways. But many of the younger were willing to try, and our scouts spent most of every day drilling the volunteers in the fashioning and use of the weapons. They also spent some time discussing various methods of organization.

Sometime later I received an encouraging report from our scouts. The Aelfir were becoming proficient with their weapons, the number of potential fighters grew almost daily, and they were also learning how to conduct themselves like soldiers in battle.

Though their organization was typical, there was a noticeable difference in their conduct. The soldiers of the Free Lands would shout in unison as they attacked the enemy. Their battle cry would celebrate the Keep for which they fought. "Honor is thrust upon you!" or "Justice is served upon you!"

The Aelfir would utter no such cry. Their attack was silent and grim.

It was my hope—though a slim one—that when the confrontation with the Kursh finally came about, some kind of organized fighting force might come from Aelf and the Kursh would find themselves assaulted by an army they had never expected.

Lars received occasional updates on these efforts and I wanted to know as much as possible. Also, I'd had the three leaders on the western edge of the Free Lands explore the possibility of recruiting fighting forces from their original native lands. Not so much mercenaries as new residents required to earn their place. If our effort was successful (and the Prophecy said that it would be) then the entire land of the Kursh would be available for settlement. These and other matters were concerns I needed to address and review.

Lucas shared what information he had early in the morning, and then he and his guard returned to Justice Keep. He was eager to return to the arms of his family, and he felt also that putting many miles between himself and the drug would be a very good thing.

I also spent several hours with the troops from Honor Keep, simply talking and listening, finding out what they would like or felt they needed, any new ideas for weapon refinements, and anything else they might have to contribute. Mostly it was just an afternoon of socializing and sustaining morale—theirs and mine.

Lars and I left early the next morning. We took our leave of Richard and Steven much as we had greeted them upon our arrival. They would leave together later in the day, traveling west before going their separate ways north and south. I reminded them both, as I had Lucas the day before, that the day of remembrance was in about three weeks. They were all expected to attend, of course, with their families. It had been a year since Honor Keep had had the privilege of hosting the Brotherhood and their families, and I was looking forward to it almost as much as Mother and Heather. I made no mention of the two other causes for celebration I had planned for that day. They could be surprised just as much as everyone else.

Lars and his guard split off from us about halfway through the journey, and turned to the northeast as we turned toward the southeast. We had only one conversation of any significance on the ride, and that was at parting.

"Lars, I hesitate to ask this, but I was wondering if you would do me a favor. This has nothing to do with the welfare of the Free Lands, but is totally of a personal nature."

"Collin, you are my friend. Of course I will, if I am able."

"It will be dangerous. Not for you, but for the man you send, and it must be one of your best."

"Ask."

I told him what I hoped he might do. He grinned. "Yes, that would certainly be worthwhile. I will see to it immediately upon my arrival at Fair."

"I thank you. Now, there is one other thing. Lars, I have changed my mind. I would like you to keep that cask and bottle in Fair Keep and not deliver it to Turg just yet."

"You have other plans for it? Or for me?"

"Both. First of all, when the time does come to deliver it, I would very much prefer you did not do it yourself. Assign it to your best scout."

"Odd that you would so suddenly develop concern for my safety."

"Not that so much. But if you were to be injured or killed during a duty I had requested, Heather would make my life a living hell. Besides, you are too important as a leader of men to risk on a relatively unimportant errand.

"However, there is more. I think I am going to suggest a thing that may actually be a violation of our values. It rests very much on the edge of acceptable."

"Well, are you going to tell me, or require me to guess?"

"The guessing would be amusing, but I'll show mercy. I think we will wait until the Kursh begin to amass their forces for the final conflict. Then, if possible, we will deliver the drug into one of their wells. It should serve to negate some of their abilities.

"That is, if you think you can safely keep the nasty stuff for two years without anyone even accidentally sampling from the bottle or cask."

"Of course. If nothing else, I will have a small storage room built with a locking door." He grinned hugely. "I really like that idea, Collin. Although you maintain a cheerful front, we all know that we will be outnumbered when that final battle is joined. Outnumbered by a great deal. Every little advantage we can gain will be well worth the effort."

Then we clasped hands and wished each other well. I picked up the pace and we maintained that pace as long as possible. I was eager to get home.

12

THE FIRST FOILED ATTEMPT

I WAS GREETED WITH GREAT ENTHUSIASM by the three ladies of my family, each with a different kind of kiss.

Tsha and I shared many more kisses later. That night in the darkness with our lovemaking behind us and before us, she spoke softly.

"Collin, I have used these days as you instructed, but I used the nights for thought. I have questions. It is not the place for a slave to inquire of her master. She accepts what is. But a free woman may inquire of her companion things she does not understand."

"You could have asked at any time, Tsha, and I think you know that. But if you are more comfortable now, that is fine too. Ask what you will."

"Collin, can you read minds?"

"Not yours, if that is your worry. What prompts this question?"

"It seemed to me that you could read the mind of the Kursh captain. You knew somehow of the man in the wagon. And then it seemed to me that you knew he would attack you while you listened to Daniel. Clearly you expected it. I was wondering if you somehow read his mind."

"No, not in any way you might mean that." Without revealing that I had expected assassins, I did explain how my various observations had revealed the presence of the crossbowman.

"As for the other, I often can anticipate what a Kursh will do in certain situations. It's really not that difficult; my father told me that he could do it as well, and how. I have shared that knowledge with my Brothers. How well they employ it, though, I know not.

"The Kursh culture, as you know, is much the opposite of ours. The things we think of as virtues—honor, fairness, truth, trust, justice—those things are sneered at in the Kursh culture. For them, any action, no matter what, is justified by the result. So in a situation with the Kursh I imagine something that I would never do because it would violate my principals, and that is the action I expect from them.

"So, yes, I expected Dort to attack with his knife when it seemed he could do so with some chance of success. I was indeed prepared. In fact, I would have been surprised if he had not attacked as he did."

She was quiet for a while. I might have thought her asleep, but her fingers continued soft caresses on my chest and shoulders. I waited.

"Collin, I have a question that is perhaps odd, for it has no importance except to satisfy my curiosity. And it is personal."

I waited.

She reached her hand to my face and stroked softly the well-trimmed beard on my cheeks and chin and throat, and rubbed her open hand affectionately across my lips.

"You are the only man I have seen in my entire life that does not shave the hairs from his face. Aelfir men do not grow whiskers. Kursh men shave every day without fail. I know, for I held a mirror for many over the years. All the men in the Keep, plus Lars and his men all were shaved. Is it some sort of badge of your authority? Or is there some other reason?"

"A few of the older men from the city that came to the Keep to see the traders sported beards or mustaches of some kind. You probably just didn't notice.

"But you are correct, too. All soldiers are required to shave daily. It is felt that it helps foster self-respect and self-discipline. The Kursh, oddly, find beards to be repulsive, except for the traders. And the general fashion in the Free Lands is indeed for the men to be clean-shaven.

"I actually wear it for vanity. I look much better with it than without it."

"Collin, I doubt that. You are as handsome, surely, as your mother and sister are beautiful."

"Thank you for the compliment. But however nature may have intended me to look, the Kursh dictated otherwise."

I had no objection to explaining, but I was going to have to step along a tight cord if I was to avoid revealing the existence of the Prophecy.

"The Kursh were given a prophecy over one hundred years ago. I have not read it, or heard how much of it there might be. But I do know one part. It says that the fourth man to hold the title of Honor of Honor Keep would be instrumental in the final defeat of the Kursh army and the resulting destruction of their culture. I am the fourth man to hold that title. The Kursh have been trying to kill me since I was ten, at least. They may have tried even earlier. Both my parents made odd references on occasion that seemed to imply that, but neither ever actually supplied details.

"When I was ten, they sent a woman. The women of the Kursh, as you know, have a greater variety of appearance than the men. If one was able to change her hair color she might pass as one from another race. This one did just that. She then took up residence at one of the hostelries in town and took odd jobs here and there. She lived there about two weeks. A Kursh would never gain access to the inside of the Keep; but in disguise she managed to get in as a temporary servant helping with outdoor preparations during a time when we had many guests. It was to prepare for my naming day celebration, which is almost funny.

"She managed to sneak into the house and hide in a closet and wait until well after night had fallen and all were asleep. She was barefoot to reduce the likelihood of being heard as she walked. Fortunately, it was quite dark. There was no moon to cast light into the room. As she approached the bed, she accidentally kicked one of the legs at the head of the bed, stubbing her toes. She inhaled sharply and actually made a small noise of pain.

"I was fortunate another way as well. She could not bring a knife—such a thing would be noticed. But she had sewn into her shirt a piece of sharpened obsidian used for scraping hides. It was more than sharp enough to cut my throat, which was what she intended.

"The combination of the jolt to the bed and the sound woke me up. I saw her stooped over me, reaching for me, and I yelled out. I also started to scoot across the bed away from her. She slashed down at my throat and across. She missed. The edge ran along my jaw, across my chin, and over my cheek to my ear.

"I yelled again and pushed the blanket up at her in defense. While she was cursing and trying to slash me again, I rolled out of bed and under it.

"Yells and footsteps could be heard outside the room. The woman cursed again. She could no longer escape through the door. She dropped to the floor and slid under the bed, still determined to slash me. But as she went under the bed on the one side, I scooted out on the other, yelling for help, and dashed for the door.

"Mother and Father were right there, and I ran into them. Father had grabbed his sword. Mother held a lit candle. The Kursh woman came out from under the bed—a trapped animal.

"She had three choices. She could surrender, she could attack, or she could—and did—jump out the window. She broke her leg on the landing. She screamed again, cursing me personally and Honor Keep as a whole, and then slit her own throat.

"My parents were upset. But when Mother saw how much blood there was on my nightclothes, the floor, and especially my face and throat, she actually screamed, then scooped me up and carried me, running down the stairs to where we attend all medical issues. You've probably seen it—a room off the kitchen with a table. After she got the blood washed off and determined exactly where the wounds were, she settled down a little. It took forever to staunch the bleeding, and I'll admit a cried a little. Partly from the pain. It hadn't hurt much when it happened—the weapon was exceptionally sharp—but the treatment hurt, and Mother crying herself made it easier for me to cry as well.

"I did hate having to attend a party in my honor with all of my lower face heavily bandaged. When I finally healed the scars were pretty ugly, I thought. I really stood out among other children, and not in a good way. Although I got used to them over the next eight years, as soon as I was able to cover them up with the beard I did so, and was somewhat pleased."

I shrugged. "Now I still stand out, but in a better way, I think."

"Was that in this room, Collin?"

"No. That room is now used by Mother as a sitting room. The blood was cleaned thoroughly off the floor that very night and the next day.

"So I like the beard. Not only does it cover the scars, but it serves to remind me of the determined treachery of my enemy."

After a long minute she kissed me, long and hard. "I like it too. It feels different from Tchon's kisses, which I still remember, and that is a good thing for me.

"I love you, Collin, as I said before, now and forever. I cannot imagine anything more wonderful than to be your wife."

She kissed me again and I returned it with an enthusiastic joy I had never felt. I wanted to laugh and shout and dance with her, spinning her around until we both fell, dizzy, to the floor. But we were both horizontal already, lying on my bed. So I kissed her on the lips, and then the throat, and then her breasts, and her stomach, and every part of her that could bring her pleasure. We made love much as we had that first night, and we held each other as tightly as we could, and we shared everything that we were.

Afterword, as we drifted off to sleep, she murmured "Thank you, my love."

"For what?"

"For everything. But specifically, thank you for answering my questions. I will answer yours tomorrow."

I was going to ask her what questions, but she was already asleep and I was falling quickly after.

13

THE KISS

THE NEXT MORNING FOR BREAKFAST Tsha requested fresh fruit, as she often did. But this time it was not only for eating. She took a pear from the bowl and handed it to me. As I held it she bent over the table to my hand and kissed the pear. Her eyes closed. I felt the movement within the fruit. When she was finished, I took my knife and sliced the pear open. All the seeds had expanded and sprouted, actually mashing the fruit around it. It no longer looked good to eat and I set it aside.

Tsha looked at me inquisitively. I grinned and nodded. "You never know what you can do until you try. Was it difficult?"

"No. It worked the very first time I attempted it, though it took a pretty long kiss. I have worked on getting it quicker and I will continue to do so."

"Excellent, Tsha. But you must tell no one about this. Not even Mother or Heather. It must remain our secret." I looked at the pear. If someone else was to see it thus, they would almost certainly think she had been demonstrating the death touch. Still, I chose not to take any chances. I sliced the thing into many pieces and personally tossed the misshapen core into the garbage bin in the kitchen. Helen gave me an odd look, but was not one to question any action I might perform. Instead, she immediately tossed a small pile of other fruit discards on top of what I'd dropped in. She looked at me without expression and I answered with a nod.

Back at the table I gave Tsha a very sincere but quick kiss. "A very good answer to question two. How about question three?"

"I am sorry, Collin, but that is not to be. I will continue to try if you wish, but once something is dead as long as the hemp fibers in rope, our gift cannot revive it."

The look of happy pride she had born only seconds before had changed to sorrow. I could not stand to see her unhappy. I took her hands and pulled her gently upright from the chair. I held her and kissed the sadness away.

"Do not sorrow over it, Tsha. It was merely a thought—a possibility to be considered. I will put it out of my mind and consider alternatives. You have done wonderfully.

"I inquired of your teacher earlier, and the answer to question one is very satisfactory. I doubt any soldier in the future will be able to take your spear from you, unless it gets lodged somehow in his innards as he falls away."

14

THE FAMILIES OF THE KEEPS

T HE PREPARATIONS FOR THE CELEBRATION were complete. With the cane crop harvested and the grain crops still in the fields the slaves usually assigned to that work acquired different duties. After the reaping shed was cleaned and closed the slaves were given different clothing and allotted duties usually reserved for the house servants.

We needed the extra help. My Brothers and their families had arrived and the guest quarters—and the guests—required attention. Unfortunately, our barracks did not have enough room for the guards accompanying the guests, so they would have to tent a quarter mile or so away from the buildings. But our kitchen would be able to do the cooking for them, though on a different schedule than what would be set for the Keep. The Brothers had been courteous enough to bring along adequate provisions to feed their soldiers. They did not, of course, insult Honor Keep by bringing along anything for themselves other than personal items.

The guests from the three Keeps in the west did not arrive together, but with a little more than an hour between arrivals. We had just enough time to properly greet one party and show them their rooms before the next family showed up.

Mother, Heather, Tsha and I stood at the gate of the Keep as each group arrived. I was proud to introduce them to my beautiful companion, and they were all sincerely pleased to meet her. Tsha performed her duties admirably. She'd been coached by her future in-laws on the formalities of the greetings and she had learned very well.

Lucas arrived first with Ruth and their son Paul. He was six and already showing that he would very much resemble his father. It was good to see Lucas looking well. He had regained some of the muscle he'd lost earlier, and his face, clean-shaven, no longer betrayed any of the ravages of the drug.

I was greeted by Ruth with an extra kiss and whispered gratitude, then she went on to greet Mother and Heather with hugs and kisses upon the cheeks and received the same.

Richard and his family arrived very shortly thereafter. Richard had no sons. His first wife, Alia, lost two children during the time she was carrying them. Doctors had told them both that a third time might prove tragic. Yet Alia had wanted so badly to fulfill, as she saw it, her duty to the Keep that she had allowed herself to become with child one more time. She was very careful and carried almost to the end, but things went bad suddenly and neither child nor mother could be saved.

Richard grieved for almost two years, and declined to pursue another woman, even though there were dozens—hundreds, probably —that would have been more than willing to marry him and bear his children.

Then he found someone. Kamilla had been of high station, but robbers had killed her husband during a business trip. Without him she was unable to support herself on the property they had purchased only the year before. Often in that situation the debtor will put themselves into slavery, their labor to pay off the debts while they are provided shelter and food.

But in this case the Brotherhood felt responsible. Those robbers were from a northern town that harbored criminals and they should have been enslaved or killed long before. Almost immediately the Brotherhood moved to correct that oversight.

They (Richard was the only one still alive that was of the Brotherhood then. The other four were the fathers of those now sworn as Brothers) had decided as a group to pay all her debts and gave her the option of working as an administrator for Center Keep, or to return debt-free to her parents' homeland. She chose the former. But during the interview, Richard found himself unexpectedly struck by her looks and her spirit.

When the gathering was officially over he stayed and courted her. The loss they shared helped to bring them together and the Brotherhood, with their families, convened again at Trust Keep barely a month later for the wedding ceremony.

I remember Father grumbling cheerfully that now they would have to find another administrator.

Richard had been unable to have sons with Kamilla, but she did give him two daughters. The oldest, Elan, was eighteen and already a fierce warrior and clearly her father's child in attitude and inclination. Her coloring was shades lighter than her father and darker than her mother but she resembled Kamilla very much in the face and figure.

She would make an acceptable heir to Trust Keep and a capable member of the Brotherhood when that time came. She and Heather were as fast as friends could be that saw each other only five or six times a year.

Elan's sister, Emilly, only a year younger, was much more like her mother in personality and ability, but resembled physically her father in color. She was not quite as close to Heather as Elan was, but she was certainly a friend. She also would make a fine heir to the title of Trust of Trust Keep if her sister somehow did not take or hold the title upon their father's death or relinquishment.

Elan also had a suitor, but she had not yet decided if she would return his affections beyond a close friendship.

Steven and Sonja, his mother, were the last to arrive from the west, though less than an hour after Trust Keep. After the formal greetings he asked too casually if Richard and his family had arrived.

Mother answered before I could, though her words were similar to what I would have offered.

"Yes, Steven, Elan is here. And she is looking especially beautiful considering the long trip and spending the night on the road. She did mention something about wanting to bathe as soon as possible. If you hurry with your own settling-in, perhaps you can find the time to join her in the chamber."

He blushed, but grinned and bowed his thanks, then tried to hurry his mother along to their quarters. Sonja, for her own amusement, came up with several little delays. After seeing her son suitably frustrated she laughed and told him to go on; the servants would make up for his slacking efforts.

He thanked her, hurried away, and we all laughed. I do not, of course, know any details, but sometime during the next night and day Steven's suit was finally accepted, and he and Elan became quite unmistakably a couple. I was pleased to note that Elan looked very happy after she had made that decision. Steven, of course, was delighted beyond any description.

Heather may have been a little disappointed that some of the precious time she'd planned to spend with her best friend was surrendered to Elan's more romantic activities. Then again, it allowed her to spend more time with Lars, so her disappointment was not too overwhelming. A few days later Mother was pleased to inform me that she witnessed the two couples often together, riding, swimming in the pools along the river, or engaging in weapons practice.

Lars and his mother and grandmother had arrived near sunset of that same day. Heather had been getting impatient as the day wore on, and she made no secret of her relief when informed that the Fair Keep visitors had arrived at the northern garrison.

Lars had brought with him an extra guest. He signaled to me that the guest was in their wagon. I distracted Tsha by insisting she spend a few extra minutes in brief conversation with Hilga and Eryn—Lars's grandmother and mother—while Lars escorted his guest from the wagon. I then asked Tsha to greet our other guest.

Tsha looked at Lars's guest, then looked again. She cried out and embraced her mother with her arms and her kisses and her tears, laughing and crying and dancing in place like an excited child ... which she was. Her mother matched her emotions, shedding tears of joy and stroking her daughter's hair and hugging her and kissing her again and again.

Tsha's mother was of course clearly Aelfir but did not look especially like her daughter. She looked older, of course, but with sharper features, more angular of nose and chin and smaller of eye. The eyes, however, were the same lavender color, and her figure was still attractive, although she seemed too thin. According to what Tsha had told me, her mother was only about forty, but she looked older. There were worry lines around her mouth and on her forehead.

After a few minutes I interrupted the reunion.

"Tsha, perhaps you would be so kind as to introduce this lady to me, and I to her?"

"Oh! Honor, I am sorry! This is my mother, Tshey. Mother, this is Honor of Honor Keep. He has been kind enough to make me his companion."

I bowed deeply. "I am blessed and pleased to meet you, Tshey. You may call me Collin if you are comfortable with that. Your daughter has accorded me the privilege of agreeing to be my companion."

She bowed in turn. "Honor of Honor Keep is a name respected in Aelf. Collin, I am blessed to meet you, and Tsha is certainly blessed to be part of your household."

"My household has been enriched by her presence." I turned to the servants waiting to show the company from Fair Keep to their quarters and carry their belongings.

"Show Fair and his company to their rooms."

I turned to Tshey. "I do apologize, but we have run out of rooms in the guest quarters. We do, however, have some extra space in the main house. Would you do us the honor of using that for your stay here?"

"The honor would be mine, Collin. Might my daughter escort me? We have much to talk about."

"Certainly. Tsha, please show your mother to that spare two-room space between Mother's and Heather's quarters. And stay with her as long as you like."

The evening meal, served shortly after the last arrivals were settled, was completely informal. Family and guests all ate in their quarters or in the dining hall, as they preferred. Servants and slaves had relocated the table with eight places to the side of the room and brought the large formal table from storage and reassembled it.

Many did in fact take their meals in their quarters, or in friends' quarters, however their social desires dictated. We did have several together in the dining hall, but few enough that we used the smaller table. Mother joined Tsha, Tshey, and I along with the three from Fair Keep. Heather did not join us. She ate with Richard's family in his rooms so that she and Elan and Emilly could catch up and fill the room with the laughter and voices of happy young women. Richard and Kamilla told me later that they could hardly get a word in edgewise and loved every minute.

Tshey's story was very much like her daughter's. Her husband, Tsha's father, Tchaik, had been killed by Kursh raiders and Tshey had been enslaved. The two of them had managed to kill five raiders before the end. This had happened within a month of Tsha's enslavement, so both women had no knowledge of the other's welfare or whereabouts.

As was the case with most of their slaves, the Kursh had used and beaten Tshey and traded her like a piece of hide between various Kursh owners over the years. In a bit of coincidence, she had been a slave in the village Lars had raided when he acquired Fia. But Tshey had been lucky. It was the policy of the Kursh to bind all slaves before battle, so that they cannot escape nor have any influence upon the outcome. Since the attack was a surprise she had not been bound. When her owner took up his weapon to fight, Tshey had fled into the woods and made her way back to Aelf. Her journey had needed more than a month to complete, and she had little to eat and very little sleep during that time, traveling through enemy land while remaining unseen by even a single Kursh.

She had been surprisingly easy to find by the man Lars had sent. She had remained in the northern section of Aelf, in one of the very few cities there. With no family, she had taken up employment in a small shop, weaving and sewing linen.

Cities were actually at that time safe from the Kursh. Turg had chosen to focus the power of his military on his plans to wipe out the military might of the Free Peoples. Kursh raiding parties had continued to harass and terrorize individual Aelf families and small settlements, but the larger population centers were not a profitable target. Then even those stopped as Turg marshalled all his forces for the invasion. I suspect that Turg planned to bring the strength of his fighting force upon the Aelf cities and towns after his enemies to the west had been destroyed.

Tshey did not know the real reason I had asked Lars to bring Tsha's family—if any could be found—to Honor Keep. She thought it was only to rediscover her daughter. I told them both that since the day of celebration was also a day of gifting, Lars and I had conspired to gift them, Tsha especially, with the visit.

Tsha did tell her mother that, though informally freed by me, her official status was still slave. That night I told her of my plans to free her officially during the day of celebration. I asked her to let it be a surprise to Tshey.

15

THE WEDDING

THE MAIN REASON FOR THE GATHERING was two days later. The stage that was reused every year was hauled out of the storage building. All the older ladies of the Keeps conspired to decorate it appropriately for the celebration. Mother did not reveal the entire schedule of events.

A small tent, high but narrow, was constructed on the surface of the stage. And, in front of that, an iron brazier filled with oiled wood. Those things were standard ceremonial apparatus for freeing a slave. I'm sure many guessed correctly which slave would be granted freedom.

The primary celebration of remembrance for my father and my assumption of the title was nothing new. I'd done it seven times before. It was stylized and formal and rather boring, except for the stark contrast of emotions. Most people celebrated my taking up of the mantle of leadership. But I and my family, and many others who had known and loved my father still felt grief in a measure equal to any feeling of happiness.

As was custom, the entire assemblage—every slave, servant, guest, and soldier save those few on duty at the garrisons—stood silent for a time, remembering someone dear that had gone on.

I thought how much I missed him still, and how I wished he'd been able to know Tsha, and to see what a wonderful woman warrior Heather had become.

Then I stepped to the front of the stage, and addressed everyone.

"Today there are other reasons to celebrate. First, let the slave from Aelf, Tsha, step onto the stage." I had told her what the ceremony entailed. I had insisted that she wear the slave linen that she wore for work in the garden and orchard.

Tsha came up from the back corner, where the steps led to the platform, and walked up to stand humbly two steps behind me. Her hands were folded in front of her and her head was down, as befitted a slave.

"She was a free woman of Aelf," I announced, "who was enslaved by the Kursh. Honor Keep was blessed with the chance to acquire her. She has increased the beauty of the Keep's garden and the production of the orchard and the fields a great deal. Her efforts and talents have greatly benefited all of the Keep, and in return she has asked nothing for herself.

"She has earned her freedom. It is now granted to her." I turned to her and extended my hand. She took it, shyly, and allowed me to guide her forward the two steps. "Tsha, you are no longer a slave. You should not dress as one."

She raised her head then and looked out at the assemblage. I noticed Tshey was in the very front with Mother and Heather. All three had tears in their eyes. Tsha nodded, then turned to the brazier and, with the small torch already burning there, she lit the wood in the brazier. The flames leaped up.

Tsha then stepped into the narrow tent. She was there for only a few minutes. When she stepped out, she was wearing the dress that had quickly become our favorite—the one she'd worn the first time she had dinner with me. Her head was up, her eyes proud and happy.

She carried her slave linens in her hands. She ceremoniously dropped first the shorts and then the shift into the brazier. She watched them burn for a moment, then turned away and stepped forward to stand next to me.

"Ladies and Gentlemen, I present to you an honored free citizen of the Keep. We are all blessed by her presence!"

The applause was loud and sincere. I let it go on for a full minute, and then raised my hand for quiet. The applause died reluctantly.

"There is one more thing yet to do." I looked to the front of the crowd. Mother, Heather, and Lars had all left their places. They reappeared on the stage, coming from the back corner. Mother held flowers. Lars bore a simple small box. I noticed that Heather walked with her hands behind her back, but I did not have time to wonder about it.

Tsha had not been told of this. When the ladies put upon her head a crown of flowers, and a bouquet was pressed into her hands, she began to understand. She looked at me with an expression of love, surprise, happiness, and a little apprehension.

Mother took her place between us and two steps behind, facing the audience. Heather gently but firmly turned Tsha so that she was facing me while Lars turned me to face Tsha. We held each other's hands.

Mother was the primary official of the Keep that was not involved, so it was her duty, and privilege, to perform the ceremony. If she or Heather were to marry at Honor Keep, the privilege would be mine.

"All, these two have expressed their wish to wed. Do any here object?" There was no response. Mother nodded and continued. "Collin, do you promise to love Tsha, to do everything in your power to keep her happy, and to allow her to do the same for you, for as long as the two of you live?"

"I do."

"Tsha, do you promise to love Collin, to do everything in your power to make him happy, and to allow him to do the same for you for as long as the two of you live?"

I felt her hands in mine. She gripped my fingers tightly to stop the trembling.

"I do."

"In accordance with the customs of the Free Lands, you are now husband and wife. Your union blesses the Lands, and the Keep, and the Keep and the Free Lands bless your union. The two of you together will always be stronger than either of you apart."

Then she looked at each of us in turn. "Gifts?"

I turned to Lars. He opened the small box and I removed the ring I had purchased for Tsha. It was a simple band, gold laced with silver. At that very instant one thought occurred to me that had not before. Tsha had no gift to give me. I should have thought of that earlier and told Mother not to ask. I could give her the ring later, in private.

Too late. I would have to give the ring now and apologize later.

I took her left hand in mine and put the ring upon her third finger. I looked into her eyes … and realized again how much I loved her and wanted her.

"Tsha, this ring is my gift to you, as a symbol of our union. Like the ring, our union will have no end."

She looked at it, stunned, then met my eyes. "It is beautiful."

Mother looked to Tsha, who turned and looked to Heather. My sister opened a box she suddenly held in front of her and Tsha took two things from it.

She turned and handed them to me. They were dark brown leather wrist guards. They would tighten with straps tied at the inside of the wrist. On the outside, each had in silver the crest of Honor Keep. I had wrist guards, but they were old and unadorned.

I held them in my hands and savored the weight and feel of them. I looked at Tsha, meeting her eyes.

"They are magnificent."

"Collin, they are sturdy and strong and represent Honor Keep, which helps protect the Free Lands, and represent also the solid strength of our love."

Mother raised her arms to just below shoulder height, open palms forward. "All, I present Collin, Honor of Honor Keep and Tsha, his bride, Lady Honor. May their union be long and fruitful!"

Finally for the first time I could kiss her publicly with no impropriety. I took her in my arms and did so. As she had every other time, she gave herself completely to me in that kiss, without reservation. I was faintly aware of the applause.

Tshey appeared on stage. She and Tsha hugged fiercely and shared kisses and happy tears and laughter. Then Tshey came to me and gave me similar treatment, with many thanks for the gift to her and her daughter.

I had consulted earlier with Mother and Heather and received their approval, in a way. Actually they threatened me with severe punishment if I did not offer. So I offered Tshey residence at the Keep, for as long as she would care to stay.

Since Tsha was living with her mother-in-law, it was only fair if I do likewise. She accepted gratefully, while warning that she might choose to return to Aelf at any time.

I didn't say anything. Although the Prophecy did not mention Tshey at all, I was positive that she would not be leaving soon, if ever. Tsha would be with child soon and there was no chance a mother would leave her daughter until after the birth. And then the chances of her leaving her grandchild after only a few months were close to zero.

Later I was able to inquire how Tsha happened to have a gift of such great value ready to present when she had not even known that the ceremony would take place.

Sometime after she had told me that she would be my wife, she had gone to Heather and Mother. She inquired about acquiring a gift for me for the coming day of gifting. She took the opportunity to accompany them both into the city. She had traded her bracelet for the guards, with guidance and advice and some hard bargaining from Mother.

Her single possession of any general value she had given up in exchange for a gift for me. I felt suddenly that I had married above my station.

That night after we made love she smiled happily. "Collin, our more precious gift is now begun. You have sired within me a son."

"Oh? How can you be certain it is not a daughter? Or even that you are so quickly with child at all?"

"For the second part, if you recall, I was absent this afternoon for some time. I prepared myself to conceive this night. It does not take long. Just as we can prevent conception, we can also assure it. As for the first, I simply know. It is what we both wish, so it will be."

I also knew that we would have a son, but my source of knowledge was more specific than hers. I did not share that knowledge with her, despite my great desire to do so. Over the next twenty-one months that small lack of sharing was one of only two tiny crumbs of unhappiness in what was otherwise the most joyful and contented time of my life.

The other crumb was my knowledge of what that damned prophecy foretold.

16

THE HEIR

A SPY CAN BE A VERY HANDY TOOL when preparing for war. I had suggested that Justice, Fair, and Honor each cultivate a spy, and that was done. It was impossible to get a spy among the Kursh. Any non-Kursh would never be trusted with any important information, not even a slave. Nor would any Kursh ever spy for any enemy.

As noted, the names of the Keeps emphasize virtues that the Free Peoples treasure, but the Kursh do not. There is no Courage Keep or Loyalty Keep. Courage and loyalty are the two virtues the Kursh treasure as much as we do.

However, I'm sure Turg was pleased to have spies in three of the Keeps. What he did not know was that Lucas, Lars, and I had actually made the spying very easy, by intention. Most of the time we simply allowed our spies to relay the information to the "secret" Kursh enclaves. That was why Dort was so certain that Tsha was at Honor Keep despite my declaration that she was not. My spy had informed the Kursh and they had sent a "trading" party to create mischief in Justice Keep and then try to acquire Tsha and/or kill me.

These spies were all half-Kursh, begotten by slave fathers and raised by their Kursh mothers with a fierce loyalty to her people. They had tried repeatedly through generations to plant these spies in the Keeps, but were always defeated. I had decided for my long-term plans that such treachery could prove useful under the correct guidance.

One month after our wedding I decided to go the safest course. I did not want the Kursh to know that Tsha was with child. While the prophecy indicated that nothing tragic would happen, I preferred to take my own measures to assure that things would proceed as foretold.

I sent my Kursh spy to Center. I told Trig that his performance had been excellent. That was true. Spy he may have been, but he pursued his servant duties with determined distinction. Our troops in Center deserved his outstanding efforts, and we needed him there for an indefinite time. I told Lars and Lucas of the move and warned them not to let anything important be known to their troops in Center Keep. I suggested that Lucas send his spy to Center as well and he agreed.

Our messages were always coded. There was too much chance that Kursh or even simple criminals might waylay our messengers. Although they rode our fastest horses and were accompanied by a single armed escort, there was always a chance the message would not be delivered.

Every message required a response. If a response was not delivered within a full day of expectation, we assumed the original was not delivered and sent a new one, this time with the added information. Actually, this did not happen often anymore. It had happened with some frequency in the years before my birth. Kursh were stopping and killing the messengers and escort almost regularly.

The Brotherhood became sufficiently annoyed that they systematically wiped out every Kursh encampment they could find. They spent almost six months on the campaign and killed well over a hundred.

Since then they tended to leave our messengers alone. Since they could not read the messages anyway they decided the risk was not worth the reward.

We were getting a response from old homelands and hundreds of warriors were trickling in from the southwest, west, and northwest. I had them all sent to Justice Keep to swell his fighting force. That was one reason I wanted Lucas's spy elsewhere. I did not want the Kursh to know that the Free Peoples were supplementing their military with outsiders.

Other than those two things I did little in the way of preparation. It was a time of waiting.

The Brotherhood met at Fair Keep and then a month later at Truth Keep. Richard and Lucas had been titled for over ten years and no longer observed the date as a holiday. But those gatherings were wonderful. We did not yet reveal that Tsha was with child. I knew that I would catch hell from the various matrons and ladies of the Keeps for not telling them, but, again, I did not want the Kursh to know too soon.

Some months later I instituted a change. When the time of gathering arrived, I encouraged the Brotherhood to bring their wives. In the case of Steven and Lars, I suggested Elan and Heather accompany us. The matrons were also welcome.

In the past, only the Brothers themselves had attended from their respective Keeps (plus their guards, of course). I felt that increased social interaction would help strengthen the unity of the Free Lands. Such strength might be quite valuable in the coming years.

The ladies were all for it, so the men had little choice but to acquiesce; in truth I doubt they had any objection. By that time Tsha was beginning to show.

Tsha was happy and proud of the demonstration of our love and mutual fertility and she wished to take her bows, as it were, among the people she respected and had come to love.

With their mothers, sisters, daughters, or wives watching—or the chief ladies of their respective Keeps—all the contestants put even more pride and focus into their efforts. Lucas was again able to participate and regained his co-championship with the javelin. There were no other changes in titles from the previous contests, but the entertainment did reach an unusual level of enthusiasm.

Other than the contests, though, Tsha was the center of interest for most of the female attendees. I was somewhat surprised to note that she seemed quite comfortable with the attention.

I do not know if an easy birth is a trait of the Aelfir, or simply a gift granted to my beautiful wife. Either way, the birth was indeed easy and the child—our son—was healthy and whole and satisfactorily loud.

She held him in her arms, cuddling and nursing him. I have never seen anyone demonstrate such pride and happiness with only the expression on her face.

"Collin, what shall we name him?"

I had thought about that quite a lot. He was unique.

"If he was your son by Tchon, Tsha, what would you have wanted to name him?"

The question startled her and she was anxiously silent for a moment.

Hesitantly, she offered, "Tchor. We had discussed possible names for boys or girls if and when. Tshel for a girl, Tchor for a boy."

"That sounds like an excellent name for our son."

"But Collin, should he not have a name more suitable for a leader of the Free Peoples? A name more in the tradition of Honor Keep?"

"Yes, I suppose he should. Tsha, I have never heard of another with the mixed parentage he has. Two names would not be too many for a child—or a man—with such a significant heritage.

"My grandfather's name was Mark. It is strong and short, and would make an excellent second name for a man of Honor Keep. If it meets with your approval, he shall be named Tchor Mark. When he grows old enough to choose, he can decide for himself which he prefers for daily use. Although unusual, having two names is not unheard of in the Free Lands."

"Collin, you have made me proud and happy with your choice. You show me again, as you do every day, why I love you so much. But in this case, my preference would be Mark Tchor. I think it has a better rhythm."

I sounded them out both ways. She was correct. When our son was announced to the world on his naming day, he was introduced as Mark Tchor, future Honor of Honor Keep.

17

THE SPY

I WAS WATCHING TSHA playing with Tchor. Odd thing—or perhaps not—but I generally called him Tchor while Tsha usually addressed him as Mark. I suspect each of us simply liked the sound of the name we preferred. Mother watched with me from the balcony. Mother and child were on the green grass at the north side of the house. Tchor was almost ten months old and trying to take his first hesitant steps while hanging on to his mother's finger. They were both smiling and laughing; happy as only a loving parent and child can be.

"Mother, do you think maybe we could just go on like this? Tsha and I raise our son in peace here in the Free Lands, and let the Kursh mind their own business?"

No answer. I turned to look at her; she was not looking at me. She was watching her grandson. She looked ... wistful perhaps. Not sad, but not happy, either.

She finally looked back at me. "Collin, you usually don't ask a question when you already know the answer."

We both sighed at the same time and watched my family.

The time of waiting was nearly over. I had summoned Trig back from Center a couple of months ago. We needed him in Honor Keep.

I congratulated myself again on not revealing what I knew to Tsha. I doubted the happiness she was enjoying would have been possible had she known of what was to come. And her happiness, conveyed to our son and shared, also fostered a happiness in me that I could barely understand, yet welcomed with gratitude.

At the same time, I had begun to share with her some of my knowledge and concerns as the commander of the armies of the Free Peoples. Our scouts had reported that Turg was beginning to amass his forces for an all-out attack on the Free Lands.

I had spread out a map of all the land of our concern—all of the Free Lands from the mountains on the west, Kursh, and Aelf, ending at the sea in the east. I had marked on it the current locations of our troops and the movements of the Kursh armies as reported. It was clear that Turg was slowly but certainly bringing his forces into a position to surge across the border between Honor Keep and Fair Keep. He was certainly aware that neither Keep had enough forces to threaten his flanks.

Turg would march his entire force right into the Free Lands. In response the Free Lands would commit all their troops from Center in a massive battle. Turg no doubt expected to win that battle with superior forces. Then with the main force of the Free Peoples dead or captured he could march his armies to each Keep, one by one, burn their fields and lay siege to each ... or even to two or three at a time depending on how many soldiers remained to him after the main battle.

Tsha was looking over my shoulder as I set the pieces on the map and voiced my conjectures.

She put her hands lightly upon my shoulders.

"Collin, why are the Kursh so against the Free Peoples? I have come to understand some of their hatred for my people. Our magic is a violation of their philosophy. But you do not threaten them or raid their borders. I could understand if they wanted to attack Honor Keep because of that prophecy. But it seems to me that it would be more reasonable if they did not aggress against you. The aggression opens the opportunity for that prophecy to be realized."

"The Kursh—and Turg especially—do not admit any belief in the inevitability of their prophecy. They have been trying to beat it for at least sixteen years now. You'd think they would learn, but they don't. It isn't in their nature to accept something like that.

"As for the other, Mother still calls it the dog and the haystack attitude."

"Dog and the haystack?"

"Yes. The story is that a dog took up residence in a field near a haystack, denning under an old and unused manger. It had no use for the haystack itself and never would, but it was close to the den. The dog would attack anything that came near the haystack. Cattle or horses might approach to feed, but the dog would attack them and chase them away. It came to regard the haystack as property and would do everything to prevent anything else from using it, even though it had no use for it.

"The Kursh regard these lands much the same way. They were in Kursh before the first of the Keeps was established. As the settlers came from the south and north and west, the Kursh tried to drive them out simply because they regarded this huge expanse of land as their own even though they have no use for it and never attempted to settle any of it themselves.

"As you know too well, Kursh is mostly forest with most of the ground not especially fit for crops. Kursh seldom farm. They hunt and fish and trade and conduct slave raids everywhere and take by force the product of the Aelfir.

"The Free Lands are a fertile area of fields and prairie with rivers and lakes and trees scattered plentifully about. There are deer and wild cattle in the land, and it is a great land for farming.

"They call us latecomers and still after many generations they seek to establish their own dominance of the land and to drive us out, or enslave us, or kill us."

I shrugged and offered a half-grin. "They are a very unreasonable people."

Tsha chuckled at that, then kissed me. "They certainly are. So, Commander, what steps will the armies of the Free Peoples take to counter this aggression?"

"I had thought that you and I would ride directly into their camp and demand that Turg take his trespassing armies back to Kursh."

I grinned again. "In the unlikely event that does not work, we will meet them in battle at a point of our choosing." I indicated a spot on the map. "We will outsmart them and outfight them and destroy them utterly."

I held my finger to my lips, and then placed a marker on the map indicating the battle site. But I placed the marker on a spot about twenty miles southwest from the location I had indicated. I winked.

Tsha looked puzzled, but nodded. I took her in my arms and kissed her and she kissed me back with the same surrender and devotion she always had. Then we left the room and went to our own rooms and made love. We took advantage of Mother's and/or Tshey's eagerness to spoil their grandson whenever we could.

"Collin, why misplace the marker?"

Before answering I went to the door, opened it, and looked around carefully. Then I closed it and went back to bed with Tsha. I spoke quietly.

"There is a Kursh spy in Honor Keep. I occasionally feed him false information without his realizing I'm giving him anything at all. He was probably listening from outside a doorway while we were talking about the Kursh plans. He will convey that false location as our true plans. One of several little details I'm planning on to help the Kursh miscalculate their final battle with the Free Peoples."

I held her close to me, skin to skin, and spoke almost directly into her ear, so quietly that even if the spy was under the bed he could not have heard.

"Lars and Lucas also have Kursh spies, and they also receive information, usually accurate but with minor details. These three spies are a vital part of our strategy.

"Tsha, I am trusting you to ignore this information as far as how you behave to everyone in the Keep."

"I will say nothing, Collin, and I will behave as I always have. Thank you for including me in your planning. Perhaps I can be of help along the way."

"I suspect you can, Tsha. In the meantime, I must make a trip to Center Keep in a week. The other four will be there. It is very important—we will discuss strategy. You'll have to stay here, along with your in-laws. And mine." I kissed her again.

18

CHE PLAN

THE BROTHERHOOD WAS IN MY QUARTERS in Center Keep. There were no curious ears lurking near the doors, and Daniel stood sentry nearby. It was his first trip away from the area of Honor Keep, and he was more eager than ever to perform well. He was not armed except with a loud voice, which would be sufficient. The windows were twelve feet above the ground and shuttered. We spoke in low voices. I was taking no chances. Our victory hinged, I felt, on what we settled in this session.

"I am sorry, Lucas, but it must be you. And there are three very good reasons."

Before Lucas could protest, Lars voiced his question. "Collin, how long have you been planning this?"

I admit I was a bit embarrassed as I answered. "About two years. Sometime before I suggested the presence of Kursh spies in the three Keeps."

"And you did not see fit to share this with the rest of us?"

"Not with anyone, Richard. Not Mother, not Halyar, even Tsha has not yet heard it. This is the first time I have voiced it aloud. And as I said, it must be Lucas."

"Why me? Collin, is this punishment for my being stupid enough to fall for the Kursh deception?"

I had to chuckle at that. "No, Brother. First, I would not do that to you. But I chose you for this long before that small incident took place. As I said, it must be you. No one else will do because no one else would."

"Collin," Richard calmly requested, "just explain your reasoning to us. You always have sound reasons for your strategies." He looked pointedly at the other three. "That is, if our Brothers will allow you to do so without interruption."

We all had to grin at that, and Lars held up his hands in surrender.

"First, as you all know, all the extra warriors that have answered our invitations have gone to Justice. Justice is the Keep closest to Center and to where the battle will be joined, so the troops will be able to get there the quickest.

"Second, Lucas has a real talent for judging the ebb and flow of battle and judging when and where best to attack.

"But the third reason is that we cannot underestimate what the Kursh know about us on a personal level. They have studied us for years—perhaps decades—and they know who we are.

"Richard is the oldest and therefore the one most dedicated to the Brotherhood. He is also the calmest and least likely to become angry enough to do such a thing.

"Steven is the youngest." I turned to him. "Steven, you are still dependent on your older Brothers for guidance and approval. This is as it should be, and was the case for all of us when we were youngest. That you would break away from us would not be credible.

"And the Kursh know very well the love that Lars and I hold for each other, and they may well know of the love he holds for my sister. They would not believe such a rift was genuine. Besides, Fair Keep is the closest to Kursh and the easiest spied upon."

I turned to Lucas. "So, Lucas, it must be you. You are older than I by a few years and it would be easily believable to outsiders that you resented my leadership enough to break your vows. There have been times that you have publicly displayed anger. And you and I have had very little social contact outside the functions of the Brotherhood. The Kursh will believe; also they will want to believe and the spies will be overjoyed to report such a rift."

I stopped and spread my hands in a gesture of near apology. "That is my reasoning. Am I in error at any point?"

Lars spoke first. "Collin, it is as I have told you several times. You think too much. You would enjoy life more if you put aside all the planning and analysis and simply followed your instincts. I would prefer we simply marshal our forces, march into that abomination of a country and kill them all. Do it before their armies have joined and are prepared for battle. Right now! Let's gather all our troops and go this very instant!"

He stopped and looked around. No one else had rallied to his speech. Richard looked faintly amused; Lucas and Steven looked uncertain and surprised.

Lars dropped his false bravado and grinned. "Well, I thought it sounded good."

"It did, except for the part you left out. If we took the fight to their land, with the disadvantage we have in numbers, we would lose and lose badly. It is a good thing, Lars, that Collin does think so much. Following your instinct would probably be the last thing we ever followed."

"Richard, Collin is right. You are too calm." Lars sighed exaggeratedly. "All right. I'm with our Commander. His plan seems very sound. Unfortunately." He favored me with another big grin.

"I do not like it, but I agree with the logic. Collin, give us the details. Not just how you see the strategy of the battle, but also how you think we should present this rift between us." Lucas favored me with a grin, then a feigned scowl. "Should I start hating you now, or wait?"

I laughed. "Please wait.

"I think it would be best if one of the spies witnessed the falling-out. I'm not sure yet which one. The other two will report separately from overheard conversation what has happened. With three independent reports, the Kursh will hopefully swallow the tale as a fish swallows the bait."

I went to the cabinet, unlocked it, and removed the map. I unrolled it on the table and the four looked upon it and the markings I had made. I then used candles, lap cloths, and a quill to demonstrate the battle strategy I had in mind.

This time it was Steven who asked the key question. "Collin, the one thing you seem to have left out is how Lucas will know when to strike."

"Steven, you are going to have to trust me on that one. The Prophecy gives us a hint. I do not yet want to share that with you. Lars knows it, and ... Richard?"

"Not in detail, Collin. I was more concerned with Edwin's part in it. I did not read beyond that more than a little."

Lars contributed, "Steven, Lucas, you don't want to know, and you really don't need to until the last minute. Just trust him. He will take care of it."

"How will he do something like that alone?"

"He will not be alone."

19

CHE BECROCHAL

L ARS ACCOMPANIED ME BACK to Honor Keep. He wished to spend some time with Heather, plus he was curious to see how "his nephew" was growing.

I had my moment. I had thought perhaps I would not, but it struck me unawares.

Lars and I were watching from a short distance. Tchor was toddling on the grass from Mother to Tsha to Heather to Tshey and back again. He was giggling; the women were laughing and cheering him on. His smile put the sun to shame.

Heather and Tsha happened to look in our direction. They smiled and waved. The love and devotion in Tsha's eyes struck me in the heart. I waved back, then turned and walked some steps away. I suppose Lars waved back to Heather, but then he joined me.

"Collin, Brother, what is it?"

"Lars, I do not want to do this." I suppose my voice was anguished, desperate. "Now that it is so close, I cannot simply take her into the chamber of execution and watch her die. Or allow her to watch me die."

Unmanly, I had allowed tears to fall from my eyes. "Lars, I love them too much. How can I take her away from her son? How can I take myself from him?" I looked at him, pleading I suppose. "I cannot do this. We will win some other way. To hell with the Prophecy!"

Lars put an arm over my shoulders. "Collin, you remember what happened last time you said that."

I sighed, raggedly, eyes on the ground before me.

"Collin, maybe you should tell her. She should know what is in store for you both, shouldn't she?"

"I will tell her. But she must make her own choices first. I will not allow that double-damned prophecy to influence her decision."

I looked at him. "You know, you really aren't a lot of comfort. You're supposed to offer me some way out of this."

He shrugged. "Sorry, Collin. You're the smart one in this alliance. You surprised me. I never believed you could have a moment of doubt. You have always been the strongest of us. If you falter, how can the rest of us deal with what is to come? Always, except that one time, you have seemed to accept what is to be, even planning your own prophesied fate. I must confess that I am nearly shocked now that you show this ... this hesitation."

"Weakness, you mean. Lars, Brother, always that fate was just an abstract. I could accept that I would die and leave Mother and Heather in grief. They are strong, and would understand, and had the prophecy to justify it all.

"I could accept leaving my son an orphan and dying with my wife—an Aelfir woman who was my slave. They were just words on paper.

"But now I look at them, I see the happiness in their eyes, the unreserved love they both give to me, and I must do this to them? You say that I am the strong one. I admit it; I am strong enough to do this because there is little choice. Our fates are decided and only the details are given to us to effect."

I looked at him, dry-eyed now. I had dropped into the depths, but with the help of his presence I had climbed out the other side. "Lars, Brother, know this. That strength is a blessing, but only because the necessity of it is a curse.

"Damn that Prophecy! Damn it, and damn the prophet to a thousand hells."

We shared silence for many minutes. Lars had turned to look again at the family. I stared off to the northwest, where Tsha and I would bring about the destruction of the Kursh.

Lars finally turned back to me. "Collin, this may not be a good time, but there never will be a better one, I think. I need something from you."

"You can help yourself to the liquor, Lars. You know that."

He grinned. "I'm glad to see you have come back to your usual self. It is more serious than that. Brother, I wish to marry your sister. I would like you to perform the ceremony as soon as possible."

I was surprised, though only by his desire that it be done so soon. "Why the rush? Lars, you two have not been needlessly careless, have you?"

'No, it's not that. At least, I don't think that is the reason. But it is her desire, so it is mine as well.

"Collin, she is right now a very junior member of the Guard of Honor, and one of your soldiers. She fears that you will insist she stay here to help defend the Keep, but also to preserve her safety. She fears that. If she is married to me she becomes a warrior of Fair Keep and will be allowed to accompany me into battle as your mother accompanied your father before you were born, and as my mother accompanied my father."

Heather knew me too well, for that is exactly what I would have done. But I knew her well, too, and knew that what Lars now requested would be the only action that would satisfy her. I did not know what Heather might do if I denied this request; I suspected that I did not want to know.

"Lars, the Free Peoples are going to need you at your very best— your most focused, at the very height of your leadership and skill as a commander and a warrior. Can you provide that without taking it upon yourself to guard one who is supposed to be guarding you?"

"That is a legitimate question. I raised that very issue with Heather myself. I was informed severely that if I could not trust her to take care of herself as she fought by my side and guarded my back, then perhaps we were not meant for each other after all."

I had to grin. "I wish I'd been witness to that. Did you prostrate yourself at her feet and beg forgiveness?"

"Not exactly. However ... I did manage to make her believe that such would not be the case. In doing so, I convinced myself as well. I do trust her, Collin, to be the warrior she needs to be. There will be no loss of focus."

"Your marriage might be very short, Brother. One or both of you might be killed. The Prophecy offers no word on that."

He nodded. "We both know that very well. The time we have together before the battle will hold joy enough to make the risk worthwhile."

I did not tell him, but I was very happy to hear that.

"We must have the wedding at Center. My spy and yours will stay in our Keeps, but Lucas will bring his to Center. It offers the perfect chance for our falling out.

"I am sorry, Brother, that we will turn a day that should be only for joy into one of conflict, even though the conflict will not be real. But I have been wondering about a good reason to get the Brotherhood together one more time so that we can stage the quarrel. This will be the perfect opportunity, and inventing another would strain credibility.

"There is just one thing. Shall I reveal the bad news? Or do you wish to tell your future bride of the discord that will seem to ruin her big day?"

He held his hands forward, palms out. "Absolutely not! It is your idea, and you must pay the price. I will get enough grief for going along with the plan.

"Besides, Collin, I will admit to my own weakness. I am very much in love with Heather. Perhaps too much. I doubt I could bring myself to cause her the grief this revelation may inspire. I do not even wish to be in the same room when she is told."

He declined to meet my eyes for several seconds, putting on a face of shame. Then he did meet my gaze.

"I would suggest, though, that you have Elizabeth close by. She may be able to restrain the violence of my beloved's response."

"Yes. That, Lars, is an excellent idea."

I looked back at the women and my son. He had tired and was sitting between his grandmothers, sleepy-eyed. He yawned. Tsha rose easily to her feet and picked him up. My son relaxed in her arms. She looked at me and signaled with her eyes that I should join her. I nodded, and Lars and I trotted over. I took Tchor from her and together we took him upstairs to his room, smiling quick farewells to the others. I noticed that Lars and Heather embraced briefly, and then walked behind us, heading for her quarters.

After we put Mark to bed we went into our own bedroom. I would have liked very much to make love with Tsha, and I think she expected that we would. But instead I sat down on a chair and told her that I was going to need to speak very seriously to Heather, and Mother would need to be present. Did Tsha wish to accompany me, or stay clear of the anger and the hurt?

She answered as I knew she would. She stood up and said, "Let's go. Whatever this is about, it should be done quickly."

When we got to Heather's quarters, I knocked. Heather's voice answered crossly that whoever it was should go away and come back next year. However, after a brief wait Lars opened the door. The two had probably been kissing, but I do not think much beyond that, judging from the neatness of their clothing and the lack of flushing in their cheeks.

With his back to Heather, Lars mouthed the word "Now?" I nodded and asked him in a low voice to fetch Mother. He turned back to Heather and kissed her hand very formally. "Love, my Commander has a duty for me and for you as well. I will see you soon." She looked unpleasantly puzzled as he turned and hurried out.

Heather glared at me. I declined to answer her glare in any way, and she was compelled to assault me verbally.

"Collin, what is this about? Did Lars talk to you about our desire to be wed? If you are going to deny me this, I will make you realize how difficult military command can be! I'll devise some way to be there, even if it means you punish me later on. I will—"

"You will be a loyal and obedient soldier of the Keep, daughter, and you will do your duty as your commander sees it!" Mother interrupted her tirade, which was fortunate. It prevented Heather from making threats she might regret later.

I closed the door, went silently to the window and looked out and below. There were no spying ears. Still I gathered us closely and spoke quietly.

I first gave Heather the good news—that she and Lars would marry in two weeks at Center Keep. She thanked me, laughing with happiness, and hugged me with a joy I hadn't felt from her in many years. Then she and Mother exchanged hugs as well.

Then I dampened their joy. I revealed that though her wedding would be joyful, the celebration afterward would be interrupted and the day would be turned into one of anger and sadness.

She actually took it better than I expected. It was Mother who challenged me on the matter. Tsha said nothing, but I could tell she also disapproved. But when I explained to them what was going to happen on the surface and what was really happening, and why, they agreed. Heather admitted that, all things considered, it was a small sacrifice I was asking and she should be glad I did not require more.

In gratitude I told her that if she liked, we would hold the ceremony in the morning and have most of the day for true celebration before the quarrel was staged late in the afternoon. That mollified her even more; then she suggested that she and Lars might even retire for the evening before we initiated the quarrel.

My response was that, unfortunately, I needed Lars present for the conflict as well as Richard and Steven, but that she could certainly be spared witnessing it if she so chose.

I left so the three ladies could start making plans. I sent a servant to find Lars and request his presence in my quarters. When he arrived, I gave him a quick recount of the conversation. I also told him, with sincere apology, that he should really head back to Fair Keep first thing in the morning. We both had plenty of arrangements to make and messengers to dispatch. I also wanted him to stay in constant contact with his scouts. We needed to stay as closely informed of Turg's preparations as possible.

He did not question or grumble but agreed immediately. It can be very difficult, I suppose, to be a commander to a best friend. I am very fortunate that Lars has always been generous with his love and cooperation. I have never taken that for granted.

"Lars," I said, as he turned to leave for his return to Heather's quarters, "it would not be proper for my sister to stay this night in your quarters. However, as my guest and very good friend, you are certainly welcome to spend the night in the house, in any room where you will find welcome."

He expressed sincere gratitude, then grinned happily and almost skipped along the corridor to the rooms of his betrothed. Shortly thereafter Tsha came into the room, shut the door, and flowed blissfully into my arms. Her lips found mine. After a very long time, she took my hand in hers and led me to the bedroom.

20

CHE RUSE

"LUCAS, WE NEED YOU TO BEHAVE a horse's ass. Sometime tomorrow evening I will reveal to Ruth what is about to happen. You must interrupt that conversation—not too soon— and act the jealous husband." I went on in some detail as to what I envisioned. He stopped me at one point.

"Collin!" He spoke urgently, but in the same very low voice I had used. We could not risk being overheard. "I cannot pull a knife on you again! The one time was twice too many!"

"It will be all right. You will not get within striking distance."

I went on at some length. I'd given this entire deception many hours of thought.

At the end he observed, "They will be reluctant. They have many friends among the other companies, and their loyalties are very much to you and the Free Peoples."

"But their loyalty is first and foremost to you. They will follow orders and withdraw. And of course your spy must be in position to witness this entire scene and hear the words."

"That will be the easiest part of this deception. I have assigned him to be my messenger, much as you use Daniel. He will always be close. The difference, of course, is that you trust Daniel with anything while I trust Seth with nothing of any importance."

"Where is he now?"

"I told him to stay with Ruth and do her bidding completely till I returned. And I asked Ruth to keep him close."

"Are you prepared to do what you will need to when he has served his purpose?"

"Prepared? Eager is the accurate term. I have no doubt he was somehow behind the Kursh targeting me with their drug. I'd have liked to kill him months ago."

I put my hands on his shoulders. "Lucas, this may be the last time we can speak as brothers. I am sorry to put this deception upon you. However, I am not sorry that the responsibility for our victory will also rest upon your shoulders. There is no one I would trust more.

"And the signal?"

"Colored smoke, you said, from their command."

"Orange or red, probably. It may be hard to distinguish among the usual white and gray, so have your soldier with the keenest eyes by your side. I hope, too, that I can lower their signal flag and keep another from going up. If you see their flag pole unadorned for long you can be certain then that the time is at hand."

"And if there is no signal, and no change in the status of the flags?"

I shrugged. "Then you will have to simply use your best judgment. Just do not be impatient. I am guessing we might be in the camp long enough for half the sand to fall through the glass before the signal can be sent. Wait at least that long unless the conditions on the field demand otherwise."

"You said 'we.' So Lars was correct. You will not be alone."

"So the prophecy has foretold."

"Does it tell if we will win?"

"Ah, Justice! As reliable as it has been all these decades, still it is only words on paper. Some answers we must provide for ourselves."

I pulled him close then and hugged him. Startled at first, he returned the embrace.

"We are Brothers, Collin, in more than just oath. May the gods be with you."

"And with you, Brother, and our armies, and all the peoples of the Free Lands."

I then turned abruptly and left. All that needed to be said was spoken. I had requested all guests to arrive at least one day early, so that I could reveal the details to the Brotherhood. After speaking to Lucas I had gathered the other three and explained their roles.

We were all able to put it aside in our minds for most of the next day. It was my honor and privilege to officiate the wedding of my sister to my best friend. The words and details of the ceremony matched that of our wedding two years before. Lars had chosen Steven to be his gift-bearer. Heather had had some difficulty choosing the lady who would stand with her and bear her gift to Lars. She had considered Tsha and Elizabeth, but Mother had an even better suggestion. Since Steven was standing for Lars, Elan would be an excellent choice to stand for Heather, especially since their friendship was of such strength and duration.

Lars followed tradition, as I had, in his choice of gifts and presented Heather with a gold ring. It was a bit larger and more ornate than the one I'd given Tsha, but still had no stone. If a warrior wears any jewelry, it is something smooth that cannot catch on any part of a weapon or be otherwise an encumbrance during battle.

Heather's gift would not fit in any box. Elan carried it wrapped in white cloth. When it was time for the exchange, Heather unwrapped it and presented it to her husband. It was a spear and one of the most beautiful weapons I have ever seen. The shaft was of polished ebony. Engraved near the tip was the symbol of Fair Keep. The tip of the spear was silver. Not only was it a magnificent symbol of leadership, but it was also a very impressive weapon. Lars was struck nearly speechless—a rare thing for him.

The feasting and celebration were enthusiastic for almost everyone, including the bride. Musicians played and the guests danced. As one might expect, the bride and groom were in high demand as dance partners. After their first dance together they were kept busy for hours with barely time to rest.

The Brotherhood put on a good face, I thought, but our minds were elsewhere. I found myself calculating when and how I could speak to Ruth alone and watching for the opportunity. I could tell the others were getting anxious.

The sun was getting low in the sky when Lucas walked with Ruth a small distance from others and stood, talking quietly. The musicians had finished their sets long since and were catching up with their dining at the tables. Richard approached, spoke quietly to Lucas for a moment, and then the two of them walked off, leaving Ruth alone. I hurried over and began speaking to her in a low voice.

Ruth was, for my tastes, not unattractive but not especially attractive either. She had long light brown hair and pretty big brown eyes, but her nose was sort of round, her face was a little to full, and she was relatively shapeless for a woman. On the other hand, she had a magnificent smile, and her personality showed through in her looks. She was a very pleasant and caring lady, and there was no doubt about the love she and Lucas shared.

She was a bit surprised that I approached her. We had had very little social interaction beyond formal greetings. This was not surprising. I had spent little social time with her husband—almost all our conversations had concerned military matters.

I spoke quickly. I had to let her know what was going to happen before it started, and Lucas's timing of his "anger" was not an exact thing.

Ruth was confused and alarmed. She had difficulty understanding what was about to happen and why. I just had time to put my hands gently on her shoulders and assure her that what she was about to see was an act, and that she should simply go with it, say little, and support Lucas.

Lucas burst on the scene at just the right instant, while my hands held Ruth's shoulders. He charged without hesitation and shoved me violently away from his wife. He cursed me and accused me of trying to come between them.

Mother, as she had in times past, anticipated what I might need. She was there along with the rest of the Brotherhood and several others. As Lucas shoved me away and then stalked after me Mother took Ruth gently aside and whispered to her. I found out later that she prevented Ruth from protesting her husband's actions and finished the explanation I had attempted.

Lucas shoved me *hard*. It was easy to respond with anger. I pushed him back hard enough that he fell backward.

"Back off, Lucas! How dare you assault your commander?"

"I dare quite well, betrayer!" He charged me again. I side-stepped and punched him in the belly. I pulled the punch but Lucas doubled over and grunted loudly. He gasped and cursed again. He glared at me, spittle around his mouth, and pulled the knife from his belt.

Their timing was perfect. Richard and Steven surged forward and each grabbed one of Lucas's arms. He struggled, cursing them both. Lars hurried forward and forcibly pried the knife from his fingers.

"Lucas!" Lars shouted, "Have you gone mad? What possesses you? Collin did nothing wrong!"

"Liar!" He shook himself, dislodging Steven and Richard from his arms. They let him go easily since he was now unarmed. "He has turned you all against me! He was trying to turn my wife, my whole family against me! His self-doubts of his leadership have finally led him to try to force me from my rightful place in the Brotherhood!"

He stopped, breathing hard. He glared at each of us in turn, saving his most venomous look for me. "Very well! If I am not respected by my so-called Brothers, then so be it! I will not be left sucking hind teat while the rest of you look down upon me or turn your backs on me!"

He walked a few steps away to stand by Ruth. Mother at that point backed away. He turned then and looked at the four of us. "I turn my back on all of you! My time with the Brotherhood is over! You have broken your vows to me, so they are no more, and there are no vows remaining. My troops will no longer be at the beck and call of the betrayer! Honor has dishonored himself and the Brotherhood! Justice is done with all of you!"

Then he took Ruth by the arm, though gently, and the two stalked away. We watched him march to his captains and speak angrily to them. They looked hesitant and regretful but did not attempt to counter his wishes even with discussion.

I took a furtive glance to the side. Lucas's spy was still there, taking in every detail.

Lars had seen him too and continued to play his role.

"Collin, what the hell was that? What business did you have with Ruth that you would not discuss with Lucas as well?"

I tried to sound bitter. "I wanted to give him a gift! Simply to show my appreciation for the devotion he has shown to regaining himself after the incident with the Kursh drugs. I was going to ask for a suggestion. I did not even get the chance. I cannot imagine what he was thinking.

"Lars, I am so very sorry that the joy of your wedding has been turned sorrowful by this. I hope Heather will forgive her older brother for this horrible turn."

"This is a very bad thing, Collin." Richard's deep voice was filled with regret and foreboding. "We cannot bear a rift in the Brotherhood. It is our strong union that has kept us safe."

Lars added, "Especially now. The Kursh are preparing for war. If Justice Keep withdraws from our union, we will have little chance. We are outnumbered even with his troops a part of our army."

"Collin," Steven urged, "you must go to him! Even though you are not in the wrong, he believes you—we—are! Apologize for the misunderstanding. Perhaps we should all go together and beg him to reconsider."

"Excellent idea, Steven. But we had best allow him some time to calm down. And perhaps Ruth can prevail upon him to reconsider. Tomorrow the four of us will go to him and humble ourselves."

Disconsolately the four of us went our separate ways, rejoining our respective families.

Mother joined Tsha and me in our quarters while Tshey, who was not privy to our schemes, took her grandson to her quarters for a nap. Which one would fall asleep first was the subject of brief debate before we spoke very quietly about the afternoon's events.

Tsha said, as she sat down on the bed, "Collin, you have angered one of your brothers to the point that he has turned his back on all of us. I have witnessed your skill with weapons. It was thrilling to see that your skill in planning deception is equally impressive. And you can even act."

"Thank you, Tsha. But it was Lucas that did the real acting. And his spy took in every word, every expression, every gesture. He's probably ready to wet his pants in his eagerness to convey that message to his contacts. But he'll have to wait to see if we can repair the damage."

"And he will be ecstatic when that attempt fails and Lucas returns angrily to Justice Keep, his troops marching in ranks behind him."

"Mother, I'm afraid his satisfaction will not last long. Shortly after Lucas is certain that his spy has betrayed him to the Kursh, he will exact the penalty for treason. And I doubt it will be clean and quick."

"What about you, Collin? What do you plan to do with your spy?"

That question took me by surprise. But Mother liked to do that every chance she got.

"What spy?"

She looked at me, eye brow raised, and waited. I looked to Tsha. She shrugged and shook her head.

"Matron, what makes you think there is a spy in Honor Keep?"

"First, 'Honor,'" she put a smirking emphasis on the title, "I know you. If you had Lucas subsidize a spy in Justice then I'm sure you would have one in Honor, and probably one in Fair as well. That is simply the way you would operate—much as your father would have. Second, I could not help but notice how careful you have been lately when discussing sensitive matters. You look out the windows, make sure the doors are closed and you speak in low tones. Obviously there is someone in the Keep that you do not trust to hear certain things. It is Trig, isn't it?"

"Have you shared these suspicions with Heather?"

"Not exactly. She shared those suspicions with me, and we discovered we'd both reached the same conclusions.

"Collin, I'm sure you felt your reasons were sound for not including us in your schemes. But you should remember that your father was also a brilliant tactician, and that Heather is just as much his child, and mine, as you are."

She smiled merrily. "She has recognized for years that you seek to protect her from the unpleasant aspects of your responsibilities. She has often grumbled to me about it. More than once I have had to persuade her not to give you a swift kick in the backside."

"Thank you for that. She has a strong foot, I suspect. But she's Lars's problem now, as well as his blessing.

"You are correct. Truthfully, I have not decided exactly what I will do with him after he has served his purpose ... but I just this second had an idea that has some appeal to it. His punishment should fit his crime.

"I think I will confront him with his treachery, than imprison him in the Keep. After the Kursh are defeated utterly in battle—

assuming my plans are as clever as I like to think they are—you can reveal to him that he was used as a dupe and his efforts on the behalf of his mother's people were instrumental in their defeat. After you have told him that you can do what you want with him."

"Collin? Why do you say suddenly that after the battle your Mother will do these things? I know you well enough to know that you would treasure the opportunity to rub his nose in his own betrayal."

I had spoken carelessly. I could not exactly lie to Tsha, but yet I still did not want her influenced by that damned Prophecy. So I shrugged.

"She will be alive and safe in Honor Keep. I might be dead. We will be seriously outnumbered by the enemy and my plans may be nothing more than self-delusion. If we do win, the cost will be very high. Of course I will be glad to deal with Trig after the Kursh are defeated—if I'm able to do so. I will admit to optimism about the final result. But I must confess to being pessimistic about myself.

"The Kursh will still try with all their might to thwart their prophecy. They will target me to a ridiculous amount. In a way that is good, since every arrow meant for me is one less meant for the warriors of the Free Peoples, and they are the ones that will do the bloody work. Every Kursh swordsman determined to slay me will be less likely to concentrate on slaying my troops.

"But with so many so dedicated to making an end of me, I do not count on that prophecy of theirs to be much protection."

Tsha reached over and put her hand upon my arm. She squeezed gently and I put my own hand over hers.

"Collin, husband, love, when we return to Honor Keep, we must talk."

Mother spoke up at once. "Do you wish to speak now? I'll be glad to leave you alone."

Tsha smiled gratefully but shook her head. "No. Our return will be soon enough. Besides, there may be more for me to learn before we have that conversation."

I probably looked a little puzzled, but I moved the conversation back to the subject at hand.

"You are also correct that there is a spy in Fair. A woman, Lars has said. After we have returned to our homes, our spies will overhear our agonized anger and grief that Justice has separated himself from the defense of the Free Lands. Our spies will rush, each separately, to inform their countrymen about this wonderful development. The word will get to Turg very quickly. He will have that information from three separate sources in three different locations. He will gleefully believe it and begin planning his after-victory campaign even before the battle is engaged.

"That is not the only bit of misinformation Trig will have supplied. Several weeks ago I carelessly left a map open in plain sight of everyone. On it I had marked, among other things, the place I had chosen where the Free Peoples would meet the Kursh in battle.

"That marked place was about a full day's march beyond where the battle will be joined. Turg and his generals will be caught by surprise, and we should be able to reduce their advantage in numbers by a significant amount in the first hour."

"What will come after that? Can you tell us?"

"I can tell you what I have planned. Whether it will come to pass is, of course, not so certain.

"We will seem to make a tactical error. After the advantage the entire army will surge forward into the very midst of the Kursh forces, apparently trying to make an early end of the battle. We will try to divide the Kursh army in two. Unfortunately we will have underestimated our enemy and we will find ourselves completely surrounded. It will seem very grim for the forces of the Free Peoples.

"All the troops Justice has at his disposal, including about five hundred that we will have held back in Center will very quietly surround the Kursh army, keeping hidden among the hills a good half-mile away from the battle. The encirclement will be thin, but the Kursh will not know that. They will only know that they are being attacked from two sides at once.

"Here is the key to the whole strategy. Turg keeps total control of his troops. He and his generals—about six that he trusts—will communicate to the captains in the field what movements they wish and the strategies they want incorporated. They communicate the same way we do: with colored flags—huge ones—raised on a pole so high that it can be seen by the entire field. I do not know what the colors will signify, except for the two universal colors, of course, white and yellow, so that opposing commanders can communicate if necessary. But like us they alter the meanings from one battle to another to keep their enemy from knowing their orders. If that communication or the decision-making can be disrupted, their efforts will lack coordination. They will simply fight in defense and continue to wait for orders to attack, retreat, or something else. And that uncertainty will weaken their will to fight. It is hard to fight with ferocity and focus when you are constantly looking to a flag pole for communication.

"It is my idea that we will disrupt their communication. I am hoping that we can leave their troops without orders. If that is accomplished Lucas will then be able to launch his attack, surprising the Kursh and forcing decisions upon Turg and his generals. If those decisions cannot be made, or cannot be communicated, then the advantage will be ours and we will destroy them all."

The ladies were quiet for a while, digesting what I had told them. Mother would not ask the question, since she knew the answer. I did not know if Tsha would notice the hole in my plan or not.

She did. "Collin, how will Lucas know that the communication has been disrupted? How will he know when to strike? For that matter, how do you propose to accomplish that interruption?"

I could but offer a wry grin. "I'm still working on that. There is a major decision to be made, yet, and it is not mine to make. When that has been done, then I will be able to put the final details together."

"Aren't you running out of time?"

"Yes. Running, but not yet out. I have confidence that all will be ready."

Mother rose, so Tsha and I did likewise. "Thank you, Collin, for letting us know what we have to expect. It sounds promising, and bleak. I remember well going into battle with Edwin, those same feelings whirling in my heart.

"It has been an eventful day. My two children are now married and my duties as mother are largely ended."

I interrupted. "But your duties as grandmother have barely begun!"

She smiled tiredly. "True enough, and I am grateful for that. But for now, I'm going to sleep. Tomorrow will be a full day as well." She kissed each of us goodnight and opened the door to our quarters and disappeared down the hall to her own rooms. When we had arrived, she had shared quarters with Heather. Now she would be alone. At home she might have furtively (or not) invited Halyar to join her. But he was in Honor Keep. She would be alone.

I closed the door behind her. When I turned around, Tsha was removing the last of her clothing. I'm sure I grinned with the delight I felt. I quickly undressed and we lay together on the bed. Sleep did come quickly to both of us ... after we expressed our love for each other in words and deeds and finally in wordless expressions of joy and ecstasy.

21

CHE PROPHEC

THE FOUR REMAINING MEMBERS of the Brotherhood were rebuffed. Lucas would not even see us; he would not hear our pleas. His messenger informed us that no one from the other Keeps was welcome anywhere within the lands of Justice Keep.

Soon thereafter he rode west, Ruth and Paul by his side. It seemed that every single warrior loyal to Justice Keep marched behind him. If any felt reluctance or sorrow they did not allow it to show in their bearing. Lucas's spy walked with the withdrawing servants and slaves. He was the only one of the entire company whose expression hinted at satisfaction. I was pretty sure I would never see him again.

Later that day Steven and Richard departed Center for their respective Keeps. They had one duty to perform before we joined together prior to battle. They would wait a full week to make sure the message from Justice was passed on to the spy's contacts and passed on from them. Then they would each, without fanfare, locate and kill every Kursh within the expanded bounds of their territories. Lucas would do likewise.

Two days later Honor's Captain Krushek along with the captains of the other three Keeps would do likewise around the expanded territory of Center, especially north, south, and east.

It seemed odd that we arrived home without Heather. She and Lars had traveled with us until it was time for them to turn north. There were tears from Mother and Heather, but happy ones, mostly.

Trig was one of the many servants to greet us when we arrived home, eager to take our belongings to our quarters and see to our requirements. Ordinarily Halyar would have greeted us as well, but we had stopped at the western garrison briefly. I had them send a message to the house garrison asking Halyar to be present at the garrison when we arrived and not to come to the house until requested.

We three changed out of our road clothing and put on casual house clothes. We would bathe later, but there was something more important to do first. Tshey continued to eagerly assume grandmother duties. She and Tchor would go immediately to the bath house. Afterward he would be allowed to play before dinner. He had slept in the wagon on the trip and was brimming with cheerful energy.

We reconvened in the dining hall. Helen brought us tea and bread. I sent Daniel to fetch Halyar. I dismissed the servants with thanks but did not assign additional duties. This allowed Trig to loiter near the doorways, where he could hear our conversations. He could claim he wished to be available immediately if needed.

Halyar was not privy to the presence of a spy in the Keep. He greeted us cheerfully, pronouncing congratulations while at the same time exclaiming how much he would miss Heather. He started to inquire if our trip had gone well—I interrupted.

"Halyar, our trip was a disaster. The wedding was fine! Do not worry about that, and Lars and Heather are quite well and very much married. But there was an incident."

I told him briefly but completely what had happened between Lucas and me, and what had resulted. I made sure that he (and Trig) understood that Justice Keep had completely withdrawn from the Brotherhood. I emphasized how bad our chances now were for the coming war with the Kursh.

Halyar looked grim. His responses were equally bleak.

"Captain, I want you to get with the sergeant, and the corporal if you think he will be of help. Before lunch tomorrow I want your best ideas of how we can successfully prosecute this war without the troops that Justice would have provided. I would like at least three different approaches."

"Yes, Honor! It will be as you say! We will begin at once!"

"Very well. We will see you tomorrow, Halyar. Please see if there is a servant within earshot."

He stepped quickly to the closest doorway. "Ah! Trig! Honor would like to speak to you."

Trig hurried in, looking as innocent and eager as a puppy.

"Yes, Honor! What do you wish?"

"Trig! Good! You will be perfect." I gestured toward a shelf on the wall. "Take one that marks an hour. You may go off duty until the sand has run out halfway. Eat, rest, whatever you like. Then report to Captain Halyar's quarters. He and others will be working into the night. Make yourself available to fetch food, drink, or whatever they might desire."

"Yes, Honor. Right away. It will be as you say."

He hurried to the shelf, grabbed a glass, turned it over, and hurried out.

"Honor, I had best hurry also. The corporal is off duty, and I will have to search him out."

I put my hand on his arm and spoke very quietly. "Just a moment, Captain. Mother?"

"Yes, Collin. I will be careful."

"Armed?"

She smiled dangerously. "Of course."

She disappeared around the corner.

"Honor? I do not understand."

"You will, Captain. I will tell you this quickly. The Matron is going to follow Trig and see where he goes and what he does. We arranged this on the ride."

"But why?"

"Trig is a spy for the Kursh. He is almost certainly going right now to relay the news to his contacts that Justice has broken from the Brotherhood, and that his forces will not be available to the Free Lands for battle."

"And the Matron is going to stop him?"

"Not at all. The Matron is simply going to make sure that he delivers the message.

"Captain, I'm afraid I have not been totally forthcoming with you. Please believe that I felt it necessary, and that it is no reflection on my regard for you or your abilities. They are the highest, and Honor Keep could not have a man better than you in your position. Elizabeth, Tsha, and Heather found out only just before we announced the schedule for the wedding.

"Halyar, Justice has not withdrawn from the Brotherhood. It was a ruse, to be reported to the Kursh by three separate witnesses—the spies present in Justice, Fair, and Honor. Turg will believe we are outnumbered even more than we are. He will also expect us to meet him in battle a full day later than we will. That is another bit of wrong information Trig acquired. I have done what I could to weaken Turg's army in a strategic sense."

He looked doubtful. "Then you do not need us to work into the night with plans?"

"Need, perhaps not. But I would still like the three of you to spend several hours on strategy and planning, just as I described. I want Trig to observe the earnestness of our concern—you must not, of course, reveal the true situation to your men.

"Besides, Captain, you are an experienced soldier and warrior, and your sergeant is also a man of great experience. I would be surprised if you do not develop something that will help us in the struggles to come."

"What of Trig, Honor? Certainly you will not allow him to simply get away with his treachery?"

I had to grin. "Do not worry yourself about that. When I have determined that he is no longer useful, he will be dealt with, and not mercifully.

"Now, my good friend, go and find the corporal. Be careful how you deal with Trig. It must be just as you always have—perhaps even more courteous than usual. But make sure he has little time to do nothing."

The captain returned my grin. "It shall be as you say. The sergeant and I have been on duty for many hours. We are quite hungry. And thirsty, too!"

He bowed and hurried from the room.

Tsha and I sat and relaxed for a short while. Then she began the conversation she had predicted earlier.

"Collin, you have said that you expect to die in the battle with the Kursh. Truly?"

I sighed, hesitated, sighed again. "Yes my love. I do truly believe that when I leave Honor Keep to lead the forces of the Free Lands against the Kursh, it will be for the last time. I will kiss Mother goodbye, and shake Halyar's hand and charge him with the duty of protecting the Keep and, incidentally, keeping the Matron satisfied and companioned, and never see either of them again.

"And I will kiss and hug our son for the final time. And I will make love to you the night before, and that also will be the final time."

"But you will not tell me goodbye. I will go with you, Collin. I will fight by your side and protect your back and live or die beside you."

"Tsha, is it not your duty, and your desire, to stay here and raise our son? I would never ask you to leave our little boy and perhaps make him an orphan."

She shook her head firmly. "No, Collin, my duty to you is to fight with you and do what I can to end the threat of the Kursh forever. I love our little boy. He has brought a joy to my life that I never imagined I could feel."

"Yes. I feel the same way. I want to just laugh with sheer happiness whenever I am with him."

"But my duty to our son is the same as yours. Your mother and Halyar will raise him, if necessary, to be the best man that he can possibly be. My mother will determine if he has our heritage, and if so she will train him in its use."

She moved her chair so that she faced me directly and so close that our knees touched. She reached forward and took my hands in hers and looked into my eyes.

"Collin, I will not be widowed by the Kursh again. I could not stand it. You are my world. If I stayed and you did not return, I would be useless as a mother. I would be only a source of sadness and loneliness and loss for Mark, and for the Keep. My presence would be much worse than my absence.

"Collin, if you die, I will die at your side, fighting. Please do not ask of me anything that would lead me to live widowed twice. I am not strong enough for that."

The pride I felt then was matched only by the love I felt for her. She had made the decision she was fated to make, and without undue influence. Her choice was honest, and from her heart. I stood up, she did likewise, and I kissed her as lovingly as I knew how, and held her in my arms for a long time. I may have shed a tear.

While we were so embraced, Mother returned. "Oh, you two, your rooms are upstairs! Surely you can wait long enough to get there!" She was grinning as she said it.

Tsha and I disengaged. "I don't see any blood."

"No. Violence was not necessary; he did not see me or hear me at all. He wrote a note on paper, then took it and ran to the stable, mounted a horse, and rode hard to the northeast. I hid and watched when he returned. He washed quickly in the servants' bath, then changed his clothing and hurried to the captain's quarters. I had opportunity to search quickly through his clothes. There was no note."

"Excellent. Thank you, Mother. We have news for you, too. There is a very good chance that your mothering duties are not over at all. Tsha has informed me that she will not remain here when the armies of the Free Lands go to meet the Kursh in battle. She refuses to be widowed a second time.

"It would seem that you and Tshey, and Halyar, will be responsible for bringing up your grandson in the ways of Honor, and also in the ways of Aelf."

"Collin, you make that sound so certain. Surely it is not that hopeless."

"My love, now that you have made that decision, and made it from your heart, there is something you must see."

We left Mother, who immediately took the opportunity to visit the bathhouse, and went up the stairs to our rooms. I went to my desk and unlocked the one drawer that was so equipped. I pulled out the scroll.

"Tsha, do you recall that I told you that the Kursh have a prophecy that I would be instrumental in the destruction of their army and their culture?"

"Of course. They have been trying to negate that prophecy since you were ten. I am very glad that they have been unsuccessful."

"That's nice to know. I'm pretty happy with that too."

I hesitated while she looked at me expectantly, wondering where this was going to go.

"Tsha, you know that I, as commander of the armies of the Free Lands as well as Honor of Honor Keep, sometimes must refrain from doing things my heart tells me, simply because my judgment so dictates. For example, I did not tell Mother or Heather about the presence of a spy for a long time. Or my plans for the ruse with Lucas until they were ready to be carried out. And they accepted those omissions because they trust me."

She nodded, still expectant.

"I hope that you will have the same acceptance, and not be angry with me for what I have not told you, even though you certainly had the right to know."

"Collin, I cannot imagine being angry with you."

"Oh? Like when I insisted that you skewer the dead Kursh in the chest or belly after he was already dead?"

She blushed, but answered firmly. "That was then. I did not then realize truly the tremendous responsibilities you live with every day; nor did I realize then the keenness of your mind. I know now that I am unbelievably fortunate to be married to the greatest man alive today. Brilliant with the bow, unbeatable with the sword, and unmatched in strategy and thought. And even a lover with a tender strength that most women could only dream about.

"I cannot imagine anything you might do, or have done, that would anger me."

"Thank you for all that. I fear your opinion of me is much too high; it is so because you love me. But I am grateful for that, because I love you. If all that you said about me is true, then I can only say that I would need to be all that to deserve to have you as my lover, my wife, and the mother of my son.

"However, enough compliments."

I indicated the scroll. "We have our own prophecy. Over one hundred years ago a man staggered out of the desert, where he had barely survived for many months on tiny sips of water and captured lizards and more than one deceived vulture. He had been a slave of the Kursh for many years, but had escaped.

"After he had recovered some of his health, he requested paper and ink. And he wrote and wrote and wrote, for months doing little else.

"At last, he was done. He presented the scroll—this scroll—to my great grandfather.

"'This is my vision of what will be,'" he told the household, "'shown to me by the desert sun and sand. It is a blessing on your house, and a curse. I am sorry for that, but it is as I have seen it. Now I must return to Kursh. I have prophecy for them as well, spoken to me by the desert nights. I must present them with it, for the two are linked.'

"He could not be persuaded to stay, or even to ride away from Kursh, so my great grandfather gave him a horse and allowed him to go the way he insisted he must. He was never seen by Honor Keep again. But many years later we did learn from Kursh prisoners that they also held a prophecy."

I opened the scroll to a well-worn spot. I knew the entire thing almost by heart, and could go to any part of it quickly. I showed her the part that I had recited to Mother after the Kursh assassins had been killed. She looked at me with an expression I could not read. "So this is why you expected them to try to kill you."

"Yes. But also, it is why I brought you to the house from the reaping shed and courted you as I did. The prophecy tells us what will happen, but not how. I tried to defeat the prophecy once. I failed, and the attempt produced only tragedy. Previous generations have also attempted to go against the dictates of this damned scroll, and all have failed, just as the Kursh have failed many times in their attempts to foil theirs.

"So now I use it when I can. Instead of fighting it, I have embraced it and plan according to what it has revealed. It tells us that Turg will attack the Free Lands as our son begins the second year of his life. That has certainly helped us to prepare for what is coming."

I unrolled the scroll further and indicated where she should start. I sat back and let her read and reread until she was satisfied. I braced myself for recriminations.

They did not come.

"Collin, I understand why you did not reveal this to me before. You wished me to make the decision to accompany you without the influence of knowing what must be. As you said, I made the decision honestly, from my heart.

"Thank you for that. And I understand now your optimism and your pessimism. But, Love, it does not say that we will die. Not exactly."

"I suppose not, exactly. But usually the phrase 'beneath Kursh weapons they will fall' means we are killed. I have never considered any other possibility."

"Then I will. It leaves room for a sliver of hope, and I will embrace that. But I told you the first time I was your dinner guest that I would gladly give my life to end the threat of the Kursh. I have not wavered in that commitment. If we die, but bring about the end of that evil terror, then my life will be complete."

I stood up and she did likewise, much as we had the first time we had confessed our love. And like that time I took her in my arms and kissed her. And like every time before, she gave me all of herself in that kiss. I realized, not for the first time, how fortunate I was.

22

ԸԷΕ SҀΟԱԸS

THREE DAYS LATER, Halyar lead a small force and wiped out every known Kursh refuge in our territory. Fair Keep did likewise.

I sent one message to Lars reminding him about the drug to be delivered to the enemy. He sent back a note stating that I was a little slow, and that his scouts had left Fair two days before with the gift.

Both Lars and I had dispatched our best scouts to track the movements of the Kursh army. It was a slow and hazardous duty. Three of my scouts and two of his never reported at all. One of Lars' scouts did report finding the headless corpse of one scout from Honor. I had to notify his family. He was not married; his parents took it hard, but well. They knew the dangers.

The other two that did not report we assumed were dead or captured. A man and a woman, both were married, but fortunately had no children and their spouses were soldiers as well.

The time had come. Turg's army began its invasion of the Free Lands.

Messages sent to the other Keeps coordinated our efforts. Truth and Trust would bring a portion of their troops to Center and all of the troops in Center, plus all reservists among the civilians of all cities and towns in the area would march east to meet the enemy at the appointed place. Lars would ride from the north and I from the south, each accompanied by only a token force. Because of our proximity to Kursh and the routes of retreat their army would take, we had to assure the protection of our Keeps.

It was time for goodbyes. I lifted Tchor and kissed him and hugged him and spun him around, lifting him high into the air until he laughed and laughed. The first anniversary of his naming day had been only two weeks before. None of the other Keeps had been able to join the celebration. All were preparing for war. But each sent a messenger with good wishes and a small gift.

I hugged Tshey goodbye, then Mother. Tsha embraced her mother and the two shed many tears. Tshey had not been told of the very probable bleak outcome, but she had picked up on the emotions of the rest of us. She suspected (but did not say) that she was going to lose her daughter again, for the last time.

"Collin," Mother said, trying to hold back the tears and present a brave face, "I have known for all of your life that this day would come. But I guess I had always thought that Heather would stand by my side and we would help each other get through it. But now I am alone."

"No you aren't. Tshey is losing her child as well. The two of you will help each other. And Halyar will help you as much as you will allow. Take care of Mark Tchor. Raise him up in the values of the Keep, and allow him his Aelfir heritage if it shows itself." We embraced again, briefly.

I turned to Halyar while Tsha and Mother embraced their goodbyes.

"Honor, I should be with you, at your side."

"No, Captain, you should not. Krushek will be there with me. I am entrusting you with the safety of my family, and of the Keep. I could not choose a better man."

I used his first name for the only time. "James, you do not need my permission to court and marry the Matron, if she is willing. But you have it, and my blessing as well." We shook hands strongly, in the warrior's way.

I turned back to Mother one last time. "Don't forget our prisoner. Keep him hungry but not starving, and when you receive word that we have won—possibly by the many Kursh soldiers fleeing back to their land—be sure to give him the punishment we discussed."

Mother bowed, smiling sardonically. "Yes, Honor. It will be as you say. Good fortune be with you both!"

Tsha and I bowed one last time, mounted our horses, and joined our waiting escort.

We would join the army of the Free Lands a day before they arrived at the designated battle site and the four commanders would see to the final coordination and placement of the troops.

I had picked a very hilly area for the battle. I hoped to be able to ambush the enemy and reduce their numbers advantage. Our best scouts and archers were scattered ahead and widely out from the Kursh route. They were to kill every Kursh scout that might warn their army of our presence. They would use knives or garrotes.

And about one day behind the combined army of the Free Lands, every available soldier under the command of Justice proceeded quietly to the site of battle.

Elan and Steven exchanged a very sincere kiss along with an equally serious embrace. Then Elan turned and embraced Heather and Tsha. There were other hugs and a few kisses (Heather and I exchanged both) as the leadership with their escorts of the Brotherhood greeted each other for what might prove to be, in some cases, the very last time.

We would meet the enemy on the field the next day. It was time to at last decide the details.

"Archers target the archers. We can hold our own with the swordsmen and the spearmen, despite their advantage in numbers. But their archers can be devastating if they gain any kind of high ground. So ours need to target theirs when the high ground is ours."

I spread out the map on a make-shift table. The commanders and their companions gathered around in a rough circle. This map was confined to the selected battle site and immediate surroundings. Hills and valleys, and the road that ran through them, were detailed.

"Truth here," I indicated the hills on the map where I wished the archers to position themselves. "Trust here, Fair over here, and Honor's archers at the fourth corner." I stopped and looked at each, inviting comment. There was none.

"Infantry will disperse similarly, but with one key difference. Truth and Fair on the flanks below their archers. Honor will take point as usual. Trust must be behind Honor and stay close and maintain a central position."

I looked at them all. "When Tsha and I go to Turg's headquarters, Trust will take command." I looked at Lars first, then Richard. Steven would understand that he was yet too young and inexperienced to have that responsibility. "Richard has the age and experience, and the patience. He will be best suited for command in that situation. But it will actually be Lucas that decides when to renew the attack. Have you agreed on the signals with Justice?" Richard nodded assent.

"Steven, this will be a firm test for you. We all know your impatience on the field. You want to kill Kursh, as many as possible. I can assure you that by day's end you will see enough of them lying on the field to satisfy your desire. But you must wait until the time is right. Also, since Richard will be occupied with the whole field we will need your vigilance to be at peak. You and your scouts must be alert for any unexpected movements or position shifts by the enemy during the lull, and communicate with Richard."

"Collin, there is one thing I do not understand. How will you and Tsha ride into Turg's camp? They are determined to kill you. How can you get there alive?"

"Good question. While I can often anticipate the actions of a single Kursh, or even a group in certain situations if face-to-face, I cannot predict what Turg will do when he is behind the battle a good quarter mile. But I am hoping that I understand him enough that my plan will work.

"The whole point of our positioning in battle is to allow them to surround us. He will be confident of victory, but not stupid. He will realize that if the Free Lands insist on fighting to the last man, his own force will be so reduced that he will be able to do nothing more than return to Kursh. He will not have nearly enough left to do anything else in the Free Lands—not even enough to lay effective siege to Fair or Honor Keeps.

"He will allow us to surrender and be enslaved. He will present the yellow flag. When I see it, I will answer with our own yellow, and the fighting will cease. He will send a messenger to escort us to his tent, with assurances that we will have safe passage. And we will have it. Turg will want to gloat and probably abuse us a little to demonstrate his superiority and glory is his presumed victory."

I sighed and took Tsha's hand in my own. I grinned half-way. "And then the two of us will, hopefully, fulfill our duty."

Tsha squeezed my hand and smiled with happy confidence. I looked around at the company.

"Questions? Complaints? Cheers?"

No response.

"You are all my Brothers, and the love and pride I hold for you knows no bounds. This may be the last time we are all together. Some of us—perhaps many of us—may die on the field tomorrow. But the Free Lands will endure." I then went to each in turn and exchanged the warrior's handshake. They all then did likewise with each other, and the company dispersed, all to join their troops and give the details of the next day's plans to their captains and sergeants.

I had one last bit of business with Lars. "Was the drug delivered?"

"Yes. My two men saw an opportunity to drug the water supply used by Turg's officers. It should afford you and Tsha a better chance."

"Excellent work! Thank them for me, Brother."

He shook his head. "I cannot. One was killed shortly after as they sought to return. The other managed to survive long enough to report success but died of his wounds."

There was nothing to say to that. I simply nodded. Lars and Heather then exchanged strong embraces with Tsha and me before parting.

Captain Krushek and his sergeants awaited us. I went through the plans and details. This was the first time I informed him that Tsha and I would probably leave the command to meet with Turg on his home field. Understandably, he was upset.

I put a hand on his shoulder. "Captain, as you know, we will be outnumbered by a great deal. The forces of Justice are in hiding about a mile away. When the battle is joined and all forces are concentrating on the fighting before them, then will his troops move into position. Tsha and I will, hopefully, disrupt Turg's communications and signal Justice when to attack. If Turg's generals are free to respond to that situation and communicate quickly to their troops, the advantage will not be ours for long. Only by keeping their fighting troops in doubt, unguided, leaderless, can we overpower their greater numbers and defeat them utterly."

I addressed him for the only time by his first name. "Louis, I have every confidence in you to lead our troops wisely and well.

Look to Fair and Trust for guidance on the timing of your counter attack. If you live through this and I do not, return to Honor Keep and the Matron will discuss with you where your duty lies. Now tell your sergeants and corporals to prepare for battle. As usual, Honor Keep will be the vanguard.

"And Captain, it has been my privilege and a blessing to Honor Keep to have your service for these many years."

His jaws were clamped tight, but he bowed stiffly. "Yes, Honor. It will be as you say." He turned and left quickly.

Tsha and I went to our tent. I secured the flap. We lay on the ground together, on our bedding, and made love for what was, I was certain, the last time. It was reminiscent of our first time, where we held each other so very tightly and poured our love into each other's hearts with our kisses and our embrace.

23

CHE ARCHERS

I TOOK MY POSITION IN THE VERY FRONT of the armies of the Free Lands. When we attacked I would hold my position until about half of my troops were before me, then my escort and I would move with them. Next to me were the flag carriers. They were three—women of about Heather's age. Their responsibilities were to keep the flag pole upright and to hoist whichever color I (or later, Krushek) commanded.

I looked upon the armies. Each soldier of Honor Keep wore a lightweight orange vest over his or her battle clothing. Beyond the orange I could see the green of Fair, the dark blue of Truth, and the light purple of Trust. Somewhere out of sight I imagined the yellow of the company of Justice. My own vest was of a darker orange—almost red.

I looked at the top of a hill a little to the south of the army, and ahead of us in the east. A lone archer/scout signaled that the enemy was barely a quarter mile before us, around that very hill. I acknowledged the signal and turned to see my Brothers. They also each signed an acknowledgment. Our archers were in place, hidden for the next moment but soon to be seen in multitudes upon the surrounding hills.

I turned to my flag carriers. "Red."

Our red flag was raised quickly to the top of the pole and I saw the same color go up on three other poles within the company. That was the sign to attack, but only after I gave the additional signal by hand.

We waited. I knew that the sergeants that commanded the archers all had their eyes on me.

The front ranks of the Kursh appeared from around the hill. They were not expecting us. I stood in the stirrups and with my saber—the ornate one of command—I swept it in a high arc over my head and pointed it at the enemy.

"Loose!" I yelled, and I saw thousands of arrows fill the air between hills and enemy. The enemy archers were still out of my site, so I could not see the devastation that was wrought. Arrows continued to fly and I saw some finally rise from the enemy and toward our own forces.

Even as I saw this I motioned again with my saber. "Forward!" I yelled, and felt the surge as my orange-clad warriors charged without hesitation to meet the enemy. After the initial advance, Tsha and I surged with them.

24

THE BATTLE

THE BATTLE HAD RAGED for over an hour. My ears rang from the sounds of metal on metal, the shouts of warriors and the cries of the wounded.

Our archers had at first devastated the bowmen of the Kursh. Then the enemy commanders raised two flags, and a large contingent of their infantry charged up the hills and attacked our archers. They suffered decimating casualties, dying not only by arrows but by thrown javelins as well. But they finally closed the distance. Our archers were now mostly dead. So were theirs, though, so our strategy had been largely successful. An occasional arrow still whistled through the air, but it was now undeniably a battle of swords and spears.

We had penetrated deeply into their ranks and found ourselves fighting on two sides. Fair on the south and Truth on the north were both hard pressed, and Richard had sent some of his force to aid both sides. Honor was more than occupied with the Kursh forces in the front.

My mind was full of images of warriors from both sides, killing and being killed. Bodies littered the field like shards of pottery. In many places the ground was muddy or slippery with blood.

I had managed to stay horsed, but Roughneck had been pierced by two arrows. He was an excellent animal and endured the arrows in his right thigh and the other in the left shoulder. He would not be running well for a long time, but he kept his feet and wheeled or stepped as directed.

Corporal Grolin had sustained an arrow in his right shoulder. Tsha had, under his direction, snapped off the shaft below the feathers, then pushed the arrow through the shoulder and pulled it out by the point on the other side. She fashioned a bandage and sling quickly from the vest of a fallen warrior. Grolin was right-handed and it was his right shoulder, but he was more than moderately able to handle a sword with his left hand.

Both of them along with others had contributed to the pile of Kursh bodies that surrounded our position. The enemy had been, as predicted, determined to get to me. I had been fortunate. Grolin had intentionally taken the arrow—it had been meant for me. I had put my own arrow into that archer's chest much as I had the Kursh that had killed Edwin. After I had signaled the charge, I had returned the saber to the scabbard and taken up the short bow.

Tsha was not yet wounded. Her skills with the spear had been exemplary. At one point the enemy had rushed a large force at me. My escort was very busy, as was I. I had had to draw the saber. It now had blood upon the blade. And two of the enemy lay dead with no external wounds.

Thousands had perished. We had had the advantage at first, but the superior numbers of the enemy were finally taking a toll. It seemed that Turg might be content to let the battle continue until virtually everyone was dead. I felt I must force his hand.

I had the two women still on flag duty (the third was dead) raise the flags signaling that we would all surge forward, no quarter, until signaled to stop. This was the signal that Steven, I knew, was hoping for. We would all focus on killing the enemy and advancing toward Turg's headquarters as quickly and determinedly as possible.

We caught the enemy by surprise. We gained nearly a hundred yards in the first ten minutes. The soldiers of the Free Lands comported themselves with courage and honor. I was incredibly proud of them all.

Then the enemy's defense stiffened, our advance halted. A messenger from Trust informed me that the Kursh had finally closed the circle behind us. Richard's forces were now fighting mostly in the back of the formation. As the casualties mounted, the armies of the Free Lands had contracted and we now occupied a relatively small area, surrounded by the Kursh on all sides.

Our army therefore presented a solid wall of warriors to the enemy. The spearmen all pushed to the front of the lines all along the perimeter. But the ground we had gained forward was significant. I instructed what few archers we had kept in the ranks, especially those with range, to send their arrows forward to the flag pole we could all see. Arrows by the dozens flew that way. It had the desired effect. Only a few minutes after the second volley landed the yellow flag appeared on the pole of the Kursh command. I quickly had our own yellow raised, the other commanders did likewise, and I could hear the shouted orders of the sergeants and corporals in our company, and the matching orders shouted by the Kursh officers as well.

The fighting ceased surprisingly quickly. I suspect all fighters on both sides were glad for the respite.

I stood up in the stirrups and caught the eye of my three commanders, reminding each one silently of their extra duties when Tsha and I left for Turg's headquarters. I received nods from all three.

The soldiers of Honor parted reluctantly, leaving a path open for the emissary from Kursh. I sat on my mount, trying to look confident and relaxed.

The mounted emissary, bearing the yellow-and-white flag of temporary truce approached me. He did not bow.

"Commander, His High Chief, Lord of the Kursh Nation and Commander of All Its Forces invites you to his tent to discuss terms of surrender."

I maneuvered Roughneck so that the emissary and I were side-by-side, facing opposite directions.

"If your commander wishes to discuss his surrender, should he not come to me himself?"

The emissary had no idea at first how to respond to that. The idea that we would expect Turg to surrender was simply incomprehensible to him. I sat and waited for him to sort out the situation and decide on a response.

"The Commander is mercifully willing to discuss the terms of *your* surrender."

"And why should we believe for one minute that we will not be killed the moment we are not surrounded by our troops?"

That time, he looked smug. "His High Chief thought you would ask that. He assures you that you will be granted safe passage to his headquarters. You have his sworn word as the ruler of the Kursh nation."

"His sworn word? The word of a Kursh? What do you have to offer that actually has value?"

He looked at first bewildered, then extremely insulted. I saved him the agony of inventing an answer.

"Forget it. We will come. You can stay. Give me the flag." I snatched the truce flag from his suddenly weakened fingers.

"Unhorse him." Three of my escort eagerly reached up and dragged him from the saddle. With a look and gesture I invited Tsha to mount the emissary's horse, and she did so, handing her spear to another of my escort. She would go unarmed.

I looked at the now standing Kursh. He looked extremely nervous. "You can be certain that if we do not return unharmed, neither will you."

I gave a nod and wink to Krushek. I leaned over to Tsha and spoke quietly in her ear with last minute instructions. Then Tsha and I rode side-by-side through the ranks of our troops, and then the enemy. That was the longest three hundred yards I'd ever ridden.

We were not molested in any way before we arrived. As predicted, a large fire burned a few yards away from the flag pole with a pile of wood nearby. There were five Kursh males huddled around a rough wooden table with a map spread out upon it. One was bloodied at the shoulder and his arm was in a sling. As I watched they passed around a skin of water and all drank deeply. A sixth general lay supine some yards away, one arrow in his neck and another in his chest.

There were perhaps a dozen others, all armed. Messengers and orderlies I supposed. There were also two women at the base of the flag pole, tending the flags. They were not armed, but their spears were on the ground nearby. The ground and even the top of the tent were littered with arrows sent from the bows of the Free Lands.

Behind the tent about a hundred yards I could see more troops—hundreds at least—that Turg was holding in reserve. This was an arrangement we had not anticipated. I could only hope that Justice had enough troops to effectively surround these reserves.

Turg was outside his tent, waiting for us.

We were invited to dismount, and we did so.

"Commander! As promised, you received safe passage to my tent, did you not?"

"Commander, we did. We have no complaints."

"Excellent." He turned to some of his men. "Tie their hands behind them and take them into my tent. I will question them there."

He turned back to me. "You and your Aelfir slave wife are now prisoners of war."

We did not protest or resist as they tied our hands. We had expected it.

As we walked to the tent I spoke to the cluster of Kursh generals and aids grouped around the table. "Be sure to check inside regularly to make sure your leader is safe. He will be outnumbered two-to-one. He might find himself in a situation he will not be able to handle."

Turg shoved us harshly into the tent, then turned to his generals. He growled, "Anyone pokes his head in there without my summons will lose it. Clear?"

"Yes, Commander," they answered in unison.

I restrained a smile. Sometimes it was almost too easy.

"Good. You have all been near to worthless as it is. Your responses and ideas have been slow and timid. If I did not know better I would swear you were all drunk!"

He stalked into the tent and then sealed the flap. It was a large tent, about twelve feet on a side. The thick center pole was at least eight feet high, and the four corner poles were about six feet. Several arrows had pierced the roof of the tent. His sleeping pallet was in the middle of the back wall. A table and single chair was nearby. The table held signs of a recent meal. Turg's command spear with the brightly decorated shaft leaned against it. We stood side by side and after the brief look around we turned toward the front, Tsha on my right. He pulled my saber from the scabbard and examined it, strutting to his right as he did so.

"A beautiful weapon, Commander. It will have a place of honor on the wall in my home in Kursh. I will accept your sword as a token of your surrender."

He started to examine the blade.

"Careful," I warned. "It is quite sharp."

He grunted dismissively, then growled wordlessly as the edge drew blood from a reckless finger.

In anger he put both hands on the hilt and drove the blade vertically into the dirt. It stuck there and remained upright, over a foot of the blade exposed between guard and ground.

I said, "Commander, there seems to be a misunderstanding. We are here as a courtesy to discuss terms of *your* surrender."

He'd been studying the small cut on his finger. When I said that he looked up at me sharply. Still angry with the saber he stepped forward and struck me with his fist from the side, smashing my cheek into my teeth and bloodying my upper lip. I was braced for it, but still I staggered to the right, bumping Tsha and staggering her, but neither of us fell.

We righted ourselves and took our previous positions. I glanced at Tsha. She looked angry but said nothing. I spit blood onto the ground.

"You will not get good terms with your surrender if you behave like that."

He started to strike me again, but then thought better of it. Instead, he laughed harshly. "You do have courage, Commander, I will grant you that. But enough with jokes. My warriors surround your armies. You are outnumbered almost two-to-one and you cannot escape. You have no real choice. If you choose to fight to the last soldier, your Lands will never recover. Your population will be so severely reduced that it will take generations to restore any kind of fighting force. My armies will easily march through and conquer your cities and Keeps, one by one."

"Commander, if we fight to the last soldier, your own force will be so reduced that you will have no chance of doing anything else. Do you not think that we all left sufficient forces at our homes to defend them?" My lip as well as the inside of my cheek continued to bleed. I spit blood again and continued, "You will be lucky to have enough of your own force left to defend your own land. It would profit you to accept our invitation. Surrender now and we will show mercy."

I had angered him again. He stepped close to me and grabbed my throat with his right hand. He squeezed, shutting off my wind.

"I will show you none, Latecomer. Surrender, or you and your slave wife will die here and now."

He looked at Tsha while continuing to choke me. "What say you, Aelfir slave? Will you die here, or should your owner save both your lives and the lives of your soldiers?"

"I have no owner. I am a free woman of the Free Lands and the Lady of Honor Keep. And if you kill him now he will be unable to surrender."

He glared at me briefly and then released his grip. I was reduced to gasping and coughing while Turg turned his back on us dismissively.

I managed to catch Tsha's eye and I gave a short nod.

After I got my breath back, I addressed Turg with contempt. "Typical Kursh. You abuse a helpless prisoner. Even with your army right outside your tent you have not the nerve to meet me in a fair duel."

"It is not a matter of nerve. It is a matter of wisdom. I have you at a disadvantage. It would be stupid of me to give that up. I know quite well of your abilities with weapons, Honor.

"So, what will it be? Save yourselves and your armies with surrender or die here with the knowledge that your second in command may do what you would not. And if he will not, then all the warriors you have out there will be killed. And we will leave their bodies where they have fallen, to let the vultures eat their eyes and tear out their hearts. The dogs will come and eat their faces, then the flies will lay their eggs in their tongueless mouths and the maggots will crawl from them."

"As they will with your dead. Commander, I will not surrender the Free Lands to you. You will have to earn your way across the Lands with Kursh blood."

He drew his sword. "Then you will die."

"Commander! May a prisoner have one last request? It is a small one."

He looked at her. "A former slave of the Kursh will be allowed to express her request."

"Allow me to kiss my husband one more time before we die? That is all. Just one last kiss."

He grinned. "You wish one last kiss? I can certainly grant that." He looked at me. "But it seems his lips are not in any shape for kissing. A kiss from me, though, you will find quite satisfactory."

She stared at him in disbelief. "You? I would rather be kissed by a wild pig. It would feel about the same."

He stepped next to her. "Your insults are brave, but stupid. You will get your last kiss from the High Chief of the Kursh nation. You should feel privileged to take that with you when you die."

He went to kiss her but she turned her head away. He gripped her hair viciously with his left hand in the back and tilted her head back. He grinned triumphantly at me.

"Turg," I warned, my teeth clenched and my voice as dangerous as I could make it, "don't. You will regret it."

He barked a harsh laugh and looked into my eyes as he forced his lips against Tsha's. It was almost too easy.

I watched closely. His eyes widened briefly then glazed over and then went dead. He collapsed at her feet.

She spat out the taste of him and stepped over the body and to me. She kissed me gently on the lips.

"You had this planned all this time? That is why you wished me to discover the death kiss?"

"Yes. It was one of several possibilities. And you did very well. I am proud of you, Tsha. Not just for now, but for all day. You have been wonderful." I kissed her, though carefully.

"Now, we must prepare to do the real dirty work." I stepped quickly to where my sword was sticking in the ground and squatted next to it, my back close. With Tsha's guidance I pressed my bonds against the blade and sawed up and down. It took only seconds for my bonds to separate. I took my knife and cut her bonds. We exchanged a hard but brief embrace.

I pulled my saber from the ground and examined it. The dirt had scratched the otherwise immaculate surface, but the edge was undamaged. Tsha stepped quickly to the rear of the tent and picked up Turg's spear.

We crept to the tent flap and I carefully opened it just enough for us to peek out. What I saw pleased me. The fire burned high. It was strangely quiet. There were no sounds of battle, and Turg's generals seemed content to sit back, drink from the water skin, and await news from Turg's tent.

We stepped back. I whispered, "We have time." We set the weapons down and I took her in my arms. We kissed long and passionately, for it was almost certainly our last one.

"Collin, I could not live without those. I am glad I will not have to."

"You have stated my own feelings, Tsha." Then I had to chuckle. "Sorry," I whispered, as I wiped my blood from her lip and chin. "But it is now our time. We will try this," and I explained what I had in mind. She simply accepted the idea and took her position. I pulled Turg's sword from his scabbard and held it in my left hand.

"Are you ready for this?"

"Yes, Love, I am ready. Let us go and fulfill that damned prophecy." She presented me with a grin as she spoke that last sentence and I could not help but return it.

I charged through the tent flaps and attacked the group around the table. A few seconds of frozen surprise, inspired by the drugged water they'd been enjoying, cost many of them their lives. The generals and aids, over a dozen in all, tried to draw their weapons even as I was upon them. I waded into them, slashing and lunging with both hands. They sought to surround me. As they concentrated on getting behind me they lost sight of the tent. Tsha emerged and without hesitation killed the two women on flag duty with Turg's spear. Then she was behind the men, thrusting once, quickly, through the ribs of one man, withdrawing the weapon and skewering another. Between the two of us we killed them all in a very short time.

We quickly shed our vests and tossed them upon the flames. We hoped that the cloth, soaked three times with the orange dye from the marigolds, would give up some of the color to the smoke.

Then we lowered the flag of temporary truce and cut the line. No other flag would be raised on that pole.

Six men were charging us from the direction we had come, swords drawn, spears held ready. Hidden by the tent, the reserves had seen nothing of what had transpired and like the troops in the front they waited to see what the next orders would command. But all too soon they would investigate the absence of orders.

The other six—no, ten—were nearly upon us. We set ourselves to meet the charge.

"I love you, Tsha."

"I love you, Collin, now and forever."

The Kursh were upon us. The killing began.

25

ᴄʜᴇ ᴄᴇɴᴄ

I HAVE TAKEN REFUGE IN THE TENT. Tsha was again magnificent. When the point of her spear lodged in the rib cage of one attacker she dropped it, dodged the point of another's spear and put her hands upon his head. She killed one more with her Defense while I killed the remainder, my own saber doing only slightly more work than Turg's weapon.

When they were all dead I picked up Tsha and carried her into the tent, stepping over a Kursh body lying in the doorway, Turg's spear protruding from his chest. She is bleeding from several wounds, but she is not dead. She was pushed backward and tripped over a Kursh body. The back of her head hit the head of a dead Kursh general. She is unconscious.

I put her gently down in a far corner of the tent where she is least likely to be disturbed by the violence that will soon begin.

I hope that damned prophet is pleased with himself.

My left leg is no longer working very well and my left arm is covered in blood, much of it my own. But it can still wield the sword.

I cannot see it, of course, but I know my back has felt the edge of the enemies' swords.

I can hear the sounds of battle. From three sides I heard the shout of the warriors of Justice as they fell upon the enemy. There was the sound of battle, too, from the east, behind the reserves, but I'd heard no shout from that quarter.

I look at my wife, my beautiful loving and beloved Tsha. I see the wounds oozing blood on her arms and legs and one very long gash in her side just below her ribs.

My vision blurs. I am not sure if it is blood or tears, but I have no time for either. I wipe the liquid from my eyes.

I see the tent flaps starting to open. I brace myself and grip my weapons. Let them come. I will kill them all.

26

CHE PROPHECY

I DID NOT KILL THEM ALL. But I did kill many. The bodies of the Kursh piled up around me and impeded the attacks of those still alive. But eventually they inflicted enough wounds upon me that my legs could no longer support me and my arms at last grew too weak to wield my saber and Turg's sword.

I find it curious that Tsha and I are still alive. We each fell beneath the weapons of the enemy, yet we did not die. She was correct in her optimism.

The number of Kursh warriors was not limitless. They finally had to forget about me and defend themselves against the warriors of the Free Lands. The reserves never did make it into the tent. They had to defend themselves against an army of Aelfir, armed with bows, arrows, and spears—simple sharpened sticks, but ones as strong and long and as sharp as any steel-tipped weapon.

I did not see it, of course, but I have been told that upon the first spilling of Kursh blood the warriors from Aelf were overcome with the same rage that had overtaken Tsha when she first used her spear upon the dead Kursh.

The Aelfir warriors died by the hundreds. But each killed at least one enemy, and often they killed two. They worked their way steadily, bloodily, through the Kursh reserves and arrived at the command tent. They found many dead Kursh and two living warriors, one of them Aelfir, and the other clearly not Kursh.

When they went to her to attend her wounds, she roused and stopped them, insisting that they see to me first.

"Tsha," I asked some days later, "Why didn't you ever tell me that the Aelfir can heal wounds?"

She looked surprised. "Collin, husband, you never asked me. Besides, it is not all of us. Only a very few have that particular gift, and it takes years of practice to be skilled enough to actually heal serious wounds in time to save lives. We are fortunate that our rescuers brought healers with them."

"Fortunate as well that they were able to fight their way to the tent." We had been lying together on our bed. We were still resting more than not. I hated it, but it was necessary. The wounds had been closed, but the muscles and tendons were slower to heal. We could walk and move normally for most things, but exertion was still beyond us. If the Aelfir healers had not attended us as soon as they did, we would probably be moving more freely, but only because our ashes would be blowing in the wind.

Many of the Kursh soldiers had fled back toward their land when it was clear they were defeated, flanking the army from Aelf. Soldiers of Honor and Fair Keeps were waiting for them. Perhaps a very few escaped. Many chose to surrender.

Every one of the Brotherhood sustained injury, but none were killed. Heather sustained two wounds, but neither one was serious.

The death toll upon the armies of the Free Lands was almost catastrophic. The Kursh, though, suffered even greater casualties. The Prophecy proved as unerringly correct in its last words as it had in all others. The Kursh nation is no more; the Kursh culture exists only in the hearts of the relatively few survivors.

The Brotherhood reconvened only a few days after the battle was over. We took stock of our losses. Messengers were sent to the Keeps. Great wagons were driven to the field and the dead were, with as much reverence as possible, loaded into the wagons and returned to their home Keeps where they would be given their final benediction by the cleansing flames of the death pyres.

We all agreed that we would leave the Kursh bodies to the appetites of nature's waste collectors for fifteen days. Then trenches would be dug, the Kursh carcasses would be thrown in and covered with dirt. It would be a nasty job. Fortunately, there were many Kursh prisoners—slaves now—that would be assigned to that task. After it was finished they would be allowed to take provisions from the stores of their army and sent across the southern desert to their original lands. To return to their homes or to the Free Lands would be punishable by death. Kursh would not make acceptable slaves for the long term. They could not be sufficiently trusted.

Steven argued against this course. He wanted us to kill them all. But the Brotherhood would not kill unarmed men and women. We are not Kursh. It is possible that someday the descendants of those we send south will return to trouble us, but that will be many generations in the future, if ever.

After supper one evening perhaps three weeks after the final victory Tsha and I were playing with Mark Tchor and I especially delighted in it. I had never expected to survive the battle and every moment that I had with my wife and son I treasured and savored and wondered at the blessing of life.

I no longer cursed the Prophecy.

Then Mother came into the room. She looked troubled. Her grandson ran to her with delight and hugged her around the knees. Her troubled expression was replaced by one of love and happiness ... but the transformation was short lived.

She had a scroll in her hands. She presented it to me then picked up Tchor and held him, receiving an enthusiastic kiss for her effort.

"Collin, I discovered this shortly after your father was killed, when I was gathering his journals to give to you. It had a note attached, instructing me that this was to be read only after the Kursh were defeated in the final battle. I elected to keep it locked up and not mention it to you at all. I had assumed that I would open it shortly after you and Tsha were given over to the pyre.

"But now you are alive, and you will raise your son. So it is for you."

I examined it closely, but there was nothing remarkable about it. It looked much like the scroll of the Prophecy, although very much smaller.

I removed the simple white cloth that bound it and unrolled it to read the beginning. I read it aloud.

"Kursh nation finally now is done
Honor four and Aelfir will raise their son
When Honor five is a young man grown
Into conflict will the Keep be thrown ..."

I stopped there and rolled up the scroll. I replaced the cloth binding, then stood and walked to the fireplace. Wood was stacked within, but not burning. I tossed the scroll onto the wood, then reached onto the mantle and took one of the burning candles. I considered for a moment, and then bent to put the candle to the wood.

"Collin! What are you doing?"

I stopped and looked at Elizabeth. "This is another Prophecy. I decline to be held prisoner again by the writing on a scroll. I thought that I would just burn it and set us all free. Perhaps if the thing no longer exists, the Prophecy, whatever it is, will also dissolve." I bent again to put flame to wood, but I was surprised. Tsha hurried forward and snatched the scroll from the wood before I could light it.

"Collin, Love, despite your hostility toward prophecy, this is too valuable to destroy. We owe too much of our happiness and the security of the Free Lands to how you used what the Prophecy foretold. This one may be at least as beneficial, especially when you apply your intelligence to its predictions."

I shrugged. "Mother, please put that cursed thing back where you've had it. We needn't bother with it for a long time—years at least."

So Mother took the scroll from Tsha. "Very well, Collin. Living without a Prophecy commanding our deeds does have great appeal. It is late. I will put this away, and then put myself to bed." She collected a goodnight kiss from her grandson and glided serenely from the room.

Mark was showing signs that he too was ready for sleep. I tossed him playfully over my shoulder which elicited the usual laughter and half-hearted kicks. We worked as a team to change him into his nightclothes and get him into bed. By the time he collected his kisses his eyes were closing against his will.

As Tsha and I undressed, she looked at me with suspicion. "Collin, you never really intended to burn that scroll, did you? It was all for show. What would you have done if neither of us had elected to grab it from the fireplace?"

I shrugged. "Drop the candle, I suppose. Or made a big show of reconsidering. But even if Mother suspects that it was just a show—and there is a good chance that she does—she will keep the thing put away in a dark drawer until we ask for it."

I kissed her. We climbed into bed and held each other close. "We deserve our time of freedom from what the future holds, and we will have it."

"As usual, you have an excellent idea. I love you, my husband, my companion, and I love the freedom you have given me and I will love the freedom that ignorance will, for a while, provide." She kissed me back with passion and we held each other very close.

Later in the night a dream awoke me. It was a dream of the long past, decades before I was born. I muttered out loud, "Great grandfather should have broken his fingers."

Tsha, curled up to my back, came awake at the sound of my voice.

"What? Break whose fingers, my love?"

"That damn prophet's. I thought I was done with prophecy, and now it seems that we will again find ourselves controlled by the words of that ancient old irritant. And, worse, our son will be in the same wagon."

Tsha kissed the back of my shoulder. "Collin, what I have seen since you told me of the Prophecy is that it does not control you, it guides you. You do not follow it, you use it. When the time comes, Mark will do the same. You will show him how."

I considered her words and realized that, as usual, she was correct. "Right again, Love. My journals will help, along with Father's."

"You have not written for a long time."

"I know. I have had other things on my mind. I did actually write down brief notes of our strategy against the Kursh and some details of the Brotherhood. I expected to die so I hurried to put down what I could.

"Now that I have time, I will write in detail everything that has happened that brought about his life and the defeat of the Kursh." I turned over to face her and kissed her softly. "You will have to help me with that. There may be things I do not recall exactly."

"And I do. Collin, obviously I cannot help with the parts when I was not present, but every conversation we have ever had, every minute that we have spent together back to when we first saw each other in the reaping shed I recall perfectly, with the clarity of the sun on a cloudless day. It will be wonderful to have that all written down for our son. He will know not only the brilliance of his father, but also the depth and breadth of the love we hold for each other."

She kissed me as I had kissed her. "Sleep now, my husband. You will have many peaceful days to write our story." She chuckled. "And I will have plenty of time to make sure you get it right."

She turned away from me and lay on her side. I could not help but laugh. I pressed myself against her back, put my arm over her and held my hand against her belly. I kissed her shoulder and allowed myself to sleep.

ABOUT THE AUTHOR

Fred Waiss was born and raised in Colorado. Once he learned the world-expanding skill of reading, he became permanently addicted. At age ten, his father introduced him to science fiction, and Robert Heinlein in particular, which led to his reading science fiction for pleasure almost exclusively for the next ten years. The "almost" means that he also read Tolkien, Howard, De Camp, and others in the fantasy genre. Like so many science fiction fans, he started writing stories as well as reading them. When possible, he writes mostly (but not exclusively) speculative fiction both as short stories and novels. He lives in Wisconsin along with his brother and one adult peculiar dog.

YOU MIGHT ALSO ENJOY

SHADOWS OF INSURRECTION

BOOK ONE OF THE UNREMEMBERED KING
by Vanessa MacLaren-Wray

Once in a generation, the matriarchs of Jeska choose a new king to manage the government and command the Guard. Corren's been training for that job since he was six, but this is an unsettled time.

BLOOD BENEATH THE SAND

by Evan Davies

Devlin Narre is a wizard, a sleuth, and a killer for hire— all to varying degrees of competence and consent.

When a routine assignment turns belly-up, it falls on Devlin to ensure that his brothers-in-arms make it out with their lives.

ENLIGHTENMENT

by Bruce Golden

Forced to leave his home, a boy learns magic from a mysterious traveling old man.

As time and distance takes him further from his home, the boy strives to learn everything he can from the old man before he dies.

Available from Water Dragon Publishing in
hardcover, trade paperback, and digital editions
waterdragonpublishing.com